His m
with

Slowly his hand moved along the fine bones of her shoulder beneath her dress.

"No Conal," she said thickly, and his hand stopped its roaming.

"You see, Catlin, you're not so different from all those other women you despise for falling for my 'meretricious charms.'"

"Did I say that?"

"Yes. The night before you left me. That's why you were so angry, wasn't it? Because you desired me in spite of the fact that you hated me. In fact, that's why you hated me."

He had it wrong, but she was not ready to confess she had been at the mercy of a passion so strong that the only way she could control it was to bury it.

ROBYN DONALD
is also the author of these

Harlequin Presents

and these
Harlequin Romances

These books may be available at your local bookseller.

For a free catalog listing all titles currently available,
send your name and address to:

HARLEQUIN READER SERVICE
1440 South Priest Drive, Tempe, AZ 85281
Canadian address: Stratford, Ontario N5A 6W2

ROBYN DONALD

return to yesterday

Harlequin Books

TORONTO • NEW YORK • LONDON
AMSTERDAM • PARIS • SYDNEY • HAMBURG
STOCKHOLM • ATHENS • TOKYO • MILAN

Harlequin Presents first edition October 1983
ISBN 0-373-10631-9

Original hardcover edition published in 1983
by Mills & Boon Limited

CHAPTER ONE

CATLIN LORING was whistling between her teeth as she unlocked her front door. It was a habit of hers when she was happy, one she indulged in with a faintly defiant air as though she half expected someone to reprimand her for it.

'That you, Catlin? Do you want coffee?' The voice belonged to Deb Munroe who shared the flat.

'Yes, please!'

Deb's black head was popped around the door into the kitchen. 'There's an airmail letter for you from New Zealand. It looks very stern and official!'

'Oh.' Catlin set her bag down on the hall table, ran a hand through her thick mane of yellow-amber hair, then walked into their small sitting room. For a moment she stared down at the envelope with its gaudy red and blue flashes with apprehensive eyes before her mouth firmed into a straight line. With fingers which trembled slightly she picked it up and opened it.

Five minutes later, when Deb came in carrying two mugs of coffee, she was still reading it, her dark brows drawn together in a frown.

'Bad news?'

'It is, rather. Conal won't release the money unless I go and see him,' she said slowly.

'Conal? I thought your lawyer was Mr Stretton?'

An odd mirthless smile curved Catlin's mouth. 'Conal is my husband.'

'Your *husband*!' Poor Deb collapsed on to the nearest chair, eyes fixed on the younger woman as if she had suddenly turned sky-blue. 'But you haven't got a husband,' she objected, curls dancing vigorously as she shook her head. 'You forget, I met you two days after you arrived in Australia. You'd just had your eighteenth birthday. You started university three weeks later and it was your first year.'

Catlin laughed without much humour, grabbing the coffee mugs just in time to prevent the contents from spilling on to the carpet. 'I remember only too vividly, idiot. I was seventeen when I married Conal——'

'Seventeen!' Deb was horrified; her eyes opened to their widest extent as they stared up at Catlin, so tall and elegant with thick lashes lowered to hide her thoughts.

'O.K.,' Deb sighed, gesturing at the chair opposite, 'put that wretched coffee down. Do you want to discuss it or shall we just continue to ignore it?'

Catlin shrugged, handed her companion one mug and lowered herself into the empty chair.

'Oh, by all means let's discuss it. I didn't tell anyone at first because the pain was too raw; later it just didn't seem to matter.'

'Not matter? Being married as a schoolgirl? I imagine it would be enough to mark you for life!'

How right you are, Catlin thought, but aloud she said calmly, 'I suppose in a way it has. For the first three years after I came to Australia everything I did was to show Conal just how wrong he was about me. I had no intention of ever seeing him again, but for my own emotional health I had to prove him wrong. He thought I was stupid, so I got a degree. He thought I was gauche and naïve beyond curing, so I jumped into instant sophistication. I learnt how to dress and how to be a hostess, I went to theatres and concerts, I read— oh, I was so determined to show him that I could be everything he thought I wasn't.'

Deb looked at her with understanding. 'So that was why you've never allowed yourself to fall for anyone. You've flirted and had fun, but no man has ever got close to you over the years.'

Catlin sighed. 'No.' A note of bitterness hardened her

voice. 'Conal likes his women experienced, but even though I was absolutely determined to prove to myself how mistaken he was about me I've never fallen into that trap. No man is going to hurt me as he did. Not ever again.'

'Why did you marry him?'

'Because I was infatuated with him.' Catlin stretched long legs before her in a movement oddly boylike and unsophisticated for one so graceful. 'It's a long story. We met on Mount Fay, my father's station in the McKenzie Basin—that's in the South Island of New Zealand. My mother died when I was a baby and except for trips like visits to the dentist I never went off the place. I had correspondence school lessons. Until I was twelve we had a housekeeper, but after she retired I ran the homestead and tried to be the son my father wanted. With a limited amount of success. But he loved me and I was perfectly happy.'

'And very innocent,' Deb observed drily.

Catlin nodded. 'Oh, a babe. Well, just after my seventeenth birthday Dad had a heart attack—rather a bad one, but he made a good recovery. Unfortunately he was convinced that he hadn't much longer to go, so he put the station on the market. He became obsessed with the idea of making my future secure; he didn't have a terribly high opinion of a woman's ability to look after herself. Looking back now, I can see that those last months must have been hideous for him. Conal Loring came up to look at Mount Fay.'

'He bought the place?'

'He did.'

'Good lord, he must have been rolling! How old is he, for heaven's sake?'

'Oh, he'd have been twenty-six then. His wife had died a year before, leaving him with a two-year-old daughter. He wasn't over her death, poor Conal. As for the money—well, the Lorings haven't had to count pennies for a hundred years or so, and not before then,

I don't think. The original settler was a younger son of wealthy English gentry. They own farms, businesses—all sorts. Conal was born rich. Mount Fay was just another business venture for him. The Lorings don't believe in keeping all their eggs in one basket—or even two or three.'

Deb sipped her coffee, watching the smooth, strong-boned face opposite with a shrewd gaze. 'Why did he marry you?' she asked after a moment.

Catlin laughed. 'Yes, you might well ask! I don't suppose even he knows that! I've come to the conclusion that he was still in an emotional vacuum caused by Claire's death—she was sick for months before she died, poor thing. It was a long-drawn-out, painful process. I'm sure that he just couldn't think what else to do with me. You see, my father had another heart attack just after the papers were signed, fatal this time, and before he died he made a new will appointing Conal my trustee.'

'He liked him that much?'

A slight grimace made Catlin look cynical. 'Conal is the sort of man other men instinctively trust. So there I was, a few months past seventeen and a real hick, with all of this money which he was responsible for until I was twenty-five. Apparently the only thing he could think of to do with me was to marry me!'

'It sounds to me as though he liked all that money,' Deb suggested suspiciously.

A slight shrug lifted Catlin's shoulders. 'Perhaps, although he certainly doesn't need it. No, I think you're wrong there. He has the kind of hard integrity that has edges so sharp it cuts you.'

'What does he look like?'

'The feverish ravings of a lovesick adolescent,' Catlin told her crisply, and burst into laughter at her friend's astonishment. 'No, honestly, I mean it! About six foot two or three, though he doesn't seem that tall until you see him with other men because he's not at all clumsy or heavy in his movements. He's no giant—lean and graceful but very, very strong. Dark hair, almost black, dark brows and a devilish habit of lifting one in astonished contempt, the kind of lashes most women glue on.'

She paused, grinning, and Deb said breathlessly, 'Well, don't stop, for heaven's sake. I don't believe you, but tell me more!'

'You asked for it, and believe me, because I hate the man, I'm not flattering him! His eyes are blue, the coldest, brightest blue I've ever seen. He looks like a Spanish Grandee, or like everyone's romantic ideal of one, all angular and hawklike. Forbidding, you could say and not be too fanciful. He is quite the most handsome man I've ever seen, but it's not his looks that make the impact. He has the kind of sexual attraction that swivels heads and makes idyllically happily married women bridle and blush when he smiles at them.'

Deb drew in a deep breath, expelling it on a sigh. 'You didn't have a hope, did you?'

'Not a hope.'

A wry smile made Catlin seem older. 'We were married at my father's bedside. When Conal made no attempt to consummate it I was bewildered, but Dad died almost immediately, and what with my grief and the turmoil that followed I wasn't really capable of functioning. I was too frightened to ask. Then he brought me up to Auckland, to his enormous great house and his mother and his daughter and his wealthy, worldly friends.'

'And... You don't need to go on. I can guess what happened.'

'I suppose you can. The way he explained it to me, I should settle down, become at home there before we did anything about our marriage. I agreed, of course. I think I knew, even then, that we'd both made an awful mistake. Stupid though I was, I'd realised that he certainly wasn't anything like in love with me. It took

Emily, his mother, to point out to me that he didn't want to go to bed with me either.' She raised her glance, wry, a little amused, to meet Deb's understanding gaze. 'Yes, she was a first-class bitch. Not that I blame her as much as I did then. She was devoted to Claire, his first wife. Everyone loved her. It must have been a hell of a shock for poor Emily to be told to fashion a suitable wife for her elegant, arrogant son out of the raw material she was given.'

'I don't see why.' Deb was indignant. 'You could go anywhere in the world now and not be ashamed. You're extremely attractive, you dress superbly and your manners are impeccable.'

Catlin was touched by such frank defence. Laughing, she said, 'Perhaps, but six years ago I was big and clumsy and tongue-tied, I knew nothing about anything but high-country farming and my school subjects, and I was madly, hopelessly infatuated with a man who had to be wondering what the hell he had let himself in for.'

'Swine!'

'Oh, at first he was kind in an aloof way, but once his mother got to work even that disappeared. I just couldn't cope; it was culture shock of the worst sort. Embarrassment and a shaming feeling of inferiority and inadequacy made me more awkward and stupid, he barely spoke to me and his friends laughed at me. It must have been as totally humiliating for him as it was for me. Half the time they didn't realise that I understood their little allusions and snide remarks, but I did.'

'Thereby proving that you weren't anywhere near as stupid as they thought!'

'Dear Deb, you'd defend the devil himself!'

'I don't,' said Deb grimly, 'feel like defending your rotten husband.'

Catlin drank down the rest of her coffee and set the mug on the floor, frowning slightly. 'Well, to be quite honest, neither do I, but I'm nowhere near as bloody-minded about him as I used to be. Maturity, I suppose. It was a completely impossible situation for everybody.'

'He should have done something about it, then.'

'I've no doubt that he was working towards some sort of solution. Nothing beats Conal, or not for long.'

'But . . .?'

'But I found him with his mistress, and being naïve and gauche and without any tact, I made a scene. We had the most appalling row.' Not even to Deb could she reveal just how that row had ended. Hurriedly she went on, 'The next day I saw a lawyer, Mr Stretton. He agreed to act for me, even gave me the address of his sister over here and insisted that I stay with her when he couldn't persuade me to stay with him and his wife. I just up and left. Mr Stretton dealt with Conal. And that's the story of my life.'

'It's absolutely incredible!' Deb leaned back in her chair, eyeing her companion as though she might suddenly turn into a Jack-in-the-box. 'I remember meeting you at Miss Stretton's that first time. She told me you'd been ill, but although you were a bit pale I'd never have known that you'd had such a terrible time! You can say what you like, but it must have taken an immense amount of self-discipline to hide the ravages!'

'I think I was numb,' Catlin admitted ruefully. 'Anyway, to get back to our sheep, what the hell am I to do about this?' With a distasteful finger she pushed at the lawyer's letter.

'Has your husband not tried to contact you before?'

'No. I forbade Mr Stretton to tell him anything, but he threatened him with the police, so Mr Stretton fixed that. A policeman visited me about a month after I got here and checked up on me. Presumably his equivalent in Auckland reassured Conal that Mr Stretton hadn't murdered me and hidden me in his files.'

'I suppose that now he wants to make sure you're still O.K. Guilty conscience, perhaps?'

Catlin gave a most unladylike snort. 'Conal? Not a

hope. His reasons are inscrutable. Oh, drat the man, I suppose I'll have to go. I need that money; Darcie wants to sell the shop as soon as possible and she'll have no difficulty. It's not as though it's going to take much of a chunk out of my inheritance.'

'How will you feel about seeing him again?' Deb knew all about her friend's desire to buy a bookshop. At the moment she was curious about Catlin's reaction after six years to her extremely unsatisfactory husband.

'Conal? Oh, perfectly all right.' Mischief lit the warm depths of Catlin's eyes. 'After all, he's going to be the one who gets the shock. He won't have changed much. I have.'

Brave words which rang slightly hollow three weeks later as the Air New Zealand jet came in over the isthmus separating Auckland's twin harbours. On one side of the narrow neck of land was the Manukau with its exquisite gradations of colour, which opened across a ferocious bar on to the turbulent Tasman Sea. On the other was the Waitemata Harbour, island-sprinkled, a passageway to the enormous Pacific Ocean and the South Seas.

Now that she was back, now that Conal was only a few miles away, Catlin found herself swallowing rather fiercely. That last searing scene, the one she hadn't mentioned to Deb, came only too vividly to mind.

'No!' she exclaimed.

The stout businessman beside her looked at her in alarm. 'Are you all right?' he asked, obviously wishing he could summon a hostess to deal with what might be incipient hysteria.

'Fine,' she lied, smiling reassuringly at him.

But she had never been able to forget that final row, the only one in which Conal's cutting contemptuous tones hadn't reduced her to trembling silence. That time, that once, the humiliation had bitten so deeply into her soul that even now she could remember her shock and despair at the sight of him with his mistress, the way the scarlet-tipped hands had run so smoothly, so confidently up his bare back—the deep note of passion in his voice when he had said her name—'Belinda . . .'

They had not known that she was there, of course. She was supposed to be at the house in Auckland while Conal spent a weekend in the beach house, but she had gone up on the Sunday to ask him if there was some way in which she could learn to be a suitable wife to him.

It was the first time she had actually driven on a public road, so she had concentrated fiercely, using her excellent bump of locality to get her to the beach house as she had only been there once before.

And then she had walked in on Conal and Belinda Scargill, still in bed. Thank goodness she had stopped before either of them had realised she was there. That humiliation she could not have borne.

Afterwards she could never remember how she got home, but when Conal arrived back that night the pain and grief and outrage had coalesced into an incandescent fury that forced her to his room to have it out.

She had been so young, so young and so smirched by his careless adultery that for once she had refused to be intimidated by him, her clear young voice scathing as she told him exactly what she thought of him.

Foolhardy, to say the least of it. After five months of living in the same house she should have known better; she had experienced his anger often enough. He rarely lost his temper, but he had a tongue capable of flaying the skin from her body. She had thought that because he was in the wrong she would have the upper hand.

Thinking of it now, she smiled with wry lack of amusement. Experience had since taught her that there are none so cruel as those in the wrong!

But Conal had revenged himself with exquisite brutality, forcing her to accept him as her husband in the most primitive way. Rape—an ugly word, the act itself even uglier. Conal had raped her, scarring her for years so that even now she had difficulty in accepting her own sexuality and its effect on men.

Oh, you have a lot to answer for, she told his image as the big jet touched down. But I've cried my last tear for you.

And she smiled, because put like that it was so melodramatic. She had outgrown that childish infatuation years ago. There was no way that Conal could hurt her, not even if he was festooned in mistresses, neck-deep in them! Good luck to him, if that was what he wanted. He no longer had the power to mess up her life.

Possibly Deb was right and it was a belated attack of conscience which made him insist on seeing her. She had never been able to see behind the hard, controlled mask of his features to the cold clever brain beneath, so his emotions, his reactions were a complete mystery to her.

The one thing she did know about him was that if he was goaded far enough he reacted with a chilling ferocious violence.

Auckland was surprisingly cool. Of course, March was the first month of autumn, but usually the days were warm and sunny. Or perhaps it was just that her memory played tricks on her, colouring the weather brighter than it had really been.

She pulled her jacket about her with a slight shiver as she followed the porter up to her hotel room. It had been easy enough to keep her courage up when she was twelve hundred miles away over the Tasman Sea, but a faint, long-forgotten nausea warned her that meeting Conal again was going to be something of a trauma.

With the hard courage which she had been surprised to discover in herself she held her head high, her mouth firming into self-control. Once inside her room she found the number in the telephone directory, dialled and after a few minutes of obstinacy found herself talking to Conal's secretary.

'I'm afraid Mr Loring is in conference,' the cool, cultured voice said implacably. 'If you care to leave a message . . .'

'Ask him to ring this number, please, between four and five this afternoon.' Ignoring the slight sound of an indrawn breath Catlin gave her number, finishing with, 'It's Mrs Loring calling.'

Now the voice was bewildered but trying hard to hide it. 'Mrs Loring? Mrs Emily Loring?'

Her mother-in-law. 'No,' Catlin replied with hidden satisfaction. 'Mrs Conal Loring. Goodbye.'

Five minutes later, just as she was changing her comfortable skirt and jacket for something a little more sophisticated, the telephone rang. Smiling, Catlin blew it a kiss and thereafter ignored it, until, after a time, it stopped.

'Good. Let him fume,' she told her reflection. Her reflection grinned back at her. Humming softly, she closed the door behind her and made her way towards the elevator.

Two hours later she found herself in a shop which catered for sportswear, watching with some amusement as a middle-aged woman tried to force a very pretty girl into the sort of clothes she felt nine-year-old brunettes with enormous blue eyes should wear. She was not getting very far. Catlin felt sorry for her but had every sympathy with the girl, who, as far as she could tell, had much better taste and the strength of will to enforce it.

'It makes you look so *old*,' the woman said wearily. 'Your father wouldn't like it.'

Catlin said with gentle firmness, 'Outfits like that are all the rage in Australia.'

Two pairs of eyes viewed her with suspicion. The woman half turned away, then, apparently at the end of her tether, spoke to Catlin's reflection in one of the long mirrors.

'It looks so—so *extreme*!'

'That's because you haven't seen many of them yet.' Catlin smiled at her, recognising the age-old sisterhood of shoppers. 'Every other child will be wearing one this winter.'

'And that's what she wants, of course.'

As if resenting the fact that she was being ignored the girl moved restlessly, her great eyes fixed on Catlin. 'Are you Australian?'

'I live there.' Something about that level gaze made her uncomfortable. A very self-possessed child, this one.

'Well . . . ' the older woman conceded on a sigh. 'Oh well, I suppose so. We've been to a hundred shops, it seems to me, and this is the only one you've liked. Although *what* your father is going to say about it, I don't know.'

'Nothing.' Something flickered in the child's eyes, hardened her mouth. 'He trusts me,' she said, producing the words with a kind of defiance.

Her companion shot a swift look at her. 'Of course he does,' she said heartily. 'Right, we'll have it, then.'

Catlin smiled at them both. As she turned the child said swiftly, 'Are you here on holiday, Miss——'

'No, I'm here on business. Goodbye. Enjoy yourself in your new clothes.'

An odd little incident, the child with her cool level stare and remarkable self-possession, the woman harried and respectful. Not related, Catlin decided as she made her way back to the hotel. They didn't have that comfortable lack of awareness of each other which implies kinship.

She had tea in the lounge, enjoying herself by watching the other people who shared the room with her. This hobby of hers was perhaps rooted in the long days of her childhood when to keep loneliness at bay she had been forced to use her powers of observation and imagination.

So absorbed was she in a rigid unspeaking couple a few feet away that her name had to be spoken a second time before it penetrated her absorption. When it did she turned her head slowly, her lashes lowered so that he could not plumb the depths of her eyes.

'Conal,' she said courteously, gesturing at the chair opposite. 'Sit down. Would you like some tea?'

His gaze was hard and intensely intimidating. 'No, thank you,' he said with icy politeness. 'But I could do with a drink.'

Of course, at that instant a waiter materialised at his elbow. Waiters always did for Conal. This one took his order, then removed himself from the scene with alacrity, obviously deducing, in the uncanny way waiters have, the state of war that prevailed.

Determined not to let the advantage gained by the shock of her appearance slip away by default, Catlin said brightly, 'You haven't changed a bit.'

It was a lie. He looked older, tougher, the lines about his mouth more deeply graven, but he was still possessed of that elegant, eye-catching charisma. That would be his when he was eighty, she decided, and hid her tension with a cool meaningless smile.

'You have,' he retorted, letting his cold blue stare sweep her face and body with insolent thoroughness.

There was no way she could hide the slight flush such a bold appraisal brought to her cheeks. Allowing her anger to show as a glitter in her eyes, she said sweetly, 'Of course. I've grown up. You've just got older.'

One thin black eyebrow climbed his forehead. In the past that mobile eyebrow had meant instant paralysis for Catlin, expressing as it did the kind of disdain she dreaded. Now she was elated to realise that it only sent the adrenalin pumping a little faster into her bloodstream.

'You have indeed grown up,' he said slowly, making no effort to hide his watchfulness. 'Very satisfactorily. Where have you been?'

'In Australia.'

He nodded, leaning back into his chair. 'I guessed as much. Was it part of your revenge to make me worry myself sick over how you were managing, or was it just your normal childish thoughtlessness?'

Familiar tactics, these. Always he had managed to

manoeuvre her into a position where she was in the wrong. Not this time, however.

Calling on her maturity to hide the nervous tension which drummed through her body, Catlin said calmly, 'I didn't think you'd be in the least interested.' A small smile, aloof and mocking, 'After all, you hadn't shown any interest up until then, so if I was wrong it was an excusable mistake to make.'

Hard blue eyes surveyed her with contempt. 'So you hoped I'd squirm. Well, I did. You were totally lacking in the qualities necessary for survival, completely immature, with the outlook and emotions of a retarded schoolgirl and a schoolgirl's stupid tit-for-tat mentality.'

'Retarded?' she said judicially, frowning slightly as though considering the matter. 'Retarded, Conal? Hardly. Not when I left.'

Hard colour lay along his cheekbones while his lashes drooped low, hiding the sudden blaze of emotion her deliberately provocative words called up. Whatever he had been going to say was balked by the waiter's reappearance. He set Conal's drink down, accepted payment, then disappeared smartly with a slightly hunted look, no doubt congratulating himself on keeping out of the line of fire.

Catlin poured herself another cup of tea, hiding a sardonic smile at his speed. For the first time she was standing up to this man who was still her husband, refusing to be overawed by his cold ruthlessness. Gone were the days when she had been so tongue-tied and gauche that she had been reduced to a quivering mass of nerves, speechless, tearful at the havoc his bitter tongue wreaked. The nervousness was still there, but well hidden by a confidence so often used that it had become part of her.

Australia, I love you! she thought, made frivolous by her relief. This scheme of Conal's, for whatever reason he had proposed it, was at last making sense to her too. Facing him like this, forcing him to accept her as a responsible human being—this was the only way to free herself of his lingering influence.

'I managed,' she said, watching from beneath her lashes as he drank deeply. 'Quite adequately, on the whole. But yes, I knew you'd feel some concern. After all, it was your sense of responsibility which led to the whole farcical situation, wasn't it. I didn't let you know where I was because I didn't want to be dragged back again like a runaway slave.'

Conal glowered down at his glass, turning it a little in long, strong fingers before glancing up sharply. 'Is that how you felt?'

'The same sense of hopelessness, yes. And,' she added softly before wisdom had time to suggest caution, 'I objected violently to being made use of when the master found his bed empty.'

Those fingers tightened on the half-empty glass. After a moment he set it down, saying with glacial composure, 'I suggest we suspend hostilities until we get home. I don't want to be flung out of here for brawling.'

The image of Conal brawling was so outrageous that a faint smile relaxed her lips. He had never been one for overt displays of the strength that the superbly cut business suit hinted at, but it was definitely there. In spite of his lean elegance his shoulders were wide, and she had very good reason to remember the power of his arms and hands.

The memory hurt like bitter cold on scar tissue. Under its influence she said acidly, 'I have no intention of going home with you. Why did you drag me all the way over here, Conal?'

'To satisfy my curiosity.'

She shrugged and picked up her cup and saucer. 'As you see.'

'Yes.' Her comment gave him an excuse to look her over again, slowly, with an insinuating thoroughness which had her grabbing hard for control.

If she had learnt anything during the months she had shared his home it was that losing her temper put her at an immediate disadvantage. His icy intelligence discovered any weakness with a scalpel's precision. His merciless tongue had kept her in subjection; it was euphoric to realise that he no longer had the power to terrify her. The old inferiority complex was gone.

Of course he realised it, and of course his tactics would change. A different set of battle strategies; she could almost see him assessing this different Catlin, searching for vulnerable chinks in her armour. It would pay to remember that the war was still raging. From that first fierce glance his attitude had made it clear that he had no intention of forgiving her the humiliation her departure had caused him.

Only now there was nothing he could do about it. Unless ... slowly she put the cup and saucer back on the table, locking eyes with his.

'You're looking very fierce,' he observed softly, his gaze telling her that he liked what he saw. The charm which had snared her adolescent heart flashed forth in all its blatant strength.

At seventeen she had known nothing about men. Bowled completely over by his splendid physical presence, she had been awed by his sophistication and intelligence, hero-worshipping him from a distance. At first he had been kind, treating her as a loved younger sister, his manner a blend of teasing and affection. But as the months rolled by that had faded, been replaced by irritation and at last a cold cruelty which had killed that childish crush while leaving her totally dependent on him. And that final destructive scene and his violation of her had left her with only hatred in her heart for him.

It had faded, of course. Maturity and even her limited experience of other men had shown her just how frustrating the situation must have been for him. That final humiliating act she could not forgive, but she could understand its causes.

Now, bathed in the warmly irresistible attraction that was as much a part of him as his ruthlessness, she knew his charm for what it was, a totally unfair combination of intangibles with infinitely more effect than a sterling character and good looks combined. Other men possessed it, or an approximation of it; several had used it to try to coax her into bed. They hadn't exactly made her immune to Conal's particular brand; she could feel the acceleration of her heartbeats, the quick rush of blood through her veins at his open appreciation. That he should possess such unfair magnetism of mind and body was unfortunate, but she was determined that it should no longer be dangerous to her.

After all, she had only to remember that beneath the excitement of his personality there was a hidden violence which still frightened her in dreams. Her memories would keep her safe.

So she repeated, 'Fierce?' raising her brows as she smiled with a cool conscious irony. 'Far from it. I'm on holiday. I've settled your mind about my welfare and I'm going to take back home the money to buy me the business I want. Why should I be fierce?'

'Put like that, no reason at all. But I don't think I'd put it exactly like that.' He swallowed a little more of his drink before continuing blandly, 'Aren't you assuming too much? You should know better than to try to push me, Cat. Remember what happened the last time you did that?'

'Vividly.'

That cold probing gaze lanced across her face, focussing on the strain and lack of colour his vicious question had caused. Smiling without humour he said coolly, 'I don't know that I'm altogether sure of your welfare. You're fine-drawn, almost haggard beneath the cosmetics. You're too thin. As for the money——' he paused while her eyes flew to meet his.

With a sick certainty Catlin realised that her

suspicions of a few moments ago had been well based. The money had been bait.

'You're going to have to convince me that this shop is a good investment,' he said silkily, watching her closely for her reactions.

Her face felt stiff, like a mask. 'I have the figures,' she began, loathing him, her disappointment so great that for one appalled moment she thought she might break down.

'Why not leave it for a week? Come home with me and relax, take it easy. Your old room is ready for you, and Jenny is rather intrigued by the idea of a runaway stepmother.' His smile held all the cynicism in the world. 'Exactly the reverse of the fairy stories.'

'And your mother?' Catlin asked harshly.

'Mama?' He lifted that brow at her. 'She too is curious.'

Delivered in the blandest of voices without a hint of challenge, that was nevertheless what he had thrown at her.

'Let's get this quite straight,' she said crisply, fighting back the old sick despair she had never thought to experience again. 'Unless I stay with you my chances of getting the money I need are pretty remote. Right?'

'Crudely put and not altogether correct. Let's just say that I want to get to know this grown-up Catlin better.'

The note of sarcasm in his deep voice drove the colour from her face, but she said harshly, 'Say what you like, that's what it amounts to. And will I be expected to—er—please you, make it worth your while to release this money—*my* money?'

Something ugly showed for a moment in the depths of his eyes but was hidden before she could decipher it. His anger was palpable, cold, contemptuous, as his glance flicked her like a whip.

'You've grown into an attractive woman,' he drawled, 'but I've always demanded beauty as a requisite for my lovers. I think you can consider yourself quite safe, Cat, unless, of course, you want to sleep with me. I don't like to disappoint a lady.' The arrogant sneer brought wild colour to her cheeks as he went on, 'I remember the last time. You were sweet in your untutored way, but not habit-forming.'

The insult made her bite her lip, but she knew better than to retaliate by flinging her cup of tea at him. In a voice totally without expression she said, 'Then if I'm forced to, I'll stay with you.'

Subconsciously she had expected it. Conal was a dangerous adversary and her flight six years ago must have flicked his pride on the raw. In her conscious mind she had hoped that they would be able to meet again with cool indifference, but her instincts had warned her otherwise. Conal wanted his pound of flesh and he was in the position to enforce his conditions. So she would go with him and although it would be difficult, for she was nowhere near as strong as she had thought, she would show him and Emily Loring that she was not the stupid, demoralised little idiot whose heart they had broken. They might be able to hurt, but they no longer had the power to shatter her.

'Right.' He didn't show triumph. He didn't need to, because it would not have occurred to him that he would be defeated. Standing, he stretched out an imperative hand. 'Come on.'

Ignoring it Catlin got to her feet. 'A week, that's all.'

He smiled, the expression in his eyes hidden by the thick dark screen of his lashes. 'Just a week. After that I'll look over the figures you've brought and make a decision. What's your room number? I'll deal with the desk if you'll pack.'

Fortunately her unpacking had been confined to a few necessities; further proof, if she needed it, that she had expected something like this. As she threw them back into her case she told herself with desperate insistence that it was no more than a week. Only a week out of her life. Seven days during which she would have to watch every word and every expression and every small gesture.

She could do it. She had to. And then she would go back home and once there she would set about getting a divorce.

CHAPTER TWO

CONAL drove a Jaguar, long and sleek and extremely comfortable. Hiding a wry smile at the thought of her small Japanese runabout, ideal for her needs, but so far removed from this opulent monster that there was no basis for comparison between them, Catlin looked wearily through the window as the car swept up the Harbour bridge. Below was the marina at Westhaven with its neatly arranged rows and rows of yachts and launches overlooked by big clubhouses; ahead lay the North Shore, a peninsula thrust into the Waitemata Harbour, dominated by the volcanic island of Rangitoto across a narrow channel.

Conal lived at one end of Takapuna beach, his big double-storeyed house hidden from prying eyes at sea by enormous pohutakawa trees which grew up the low cliff. Beneath them steps led down to a little cove which was so difficult of access from the main beach that it was usually empty of sunbathers and swimmers.

At first sight nothing much had changed. Oleanders still held their crinkly silk flowers to the sky, exquisite and deadly poisonous, belladonna lilies bloomed in stately pink and white and cerise nakedness between shrubs and plants in the gardens which Mrs Loring liked to think of as being as close to an English herbaceous border as was possible in the Antipodes. The grape vine over the little summerhouse was still green, but the purple cones of fruit had been harvested. Rosemary bloomed, blue and bee-fussed, and the little shot-silk flowers of portulacas made brilliant mats in all of the warm colours of the rainbow.

Dreaming in the late afternoon sun, the house was a gracious dowager, one of the first to be built in the days when the only access to the North Shore was by ferry. A late-Victorian Loring with surprisingly advanced tastes for his time had planned it, with little of the fussy gingerbread that marred so many similar houses. Instead it relied on its lines and some elegantly curved bay windows for effect, the white weather-boarding immaculate as always.

And, as always, there was Mrs Loring at the door, small and upright, those cold blue eyes flickering over Catlin with not the slightest pretence of a welcome.

'Catherine,' she said in her clear cultured voice. 'Come in. You'll be wanting a shower, I suppose, after the flight.'

'I showered at the hotel,' Catlin told her.

Mrs Loring stared at her. 'What hotel?'

Conal, coming up behind with Catlin's bag, explained, and something in his mother's expression unfroze.

'Oh, I see. But how could you think of staying in an hotel? You must have known that your place is here?'

Smiling, allowing a note of sardonic amusement to appear in her tones, Catlin said, 'No, why? I made my opinion of this place very clear when I left it. I can assure you that the only reason I'm back is because Conal insisted on it.'

Emily's glance swung to her son's face, met its deliberate impassivity with anger.

'I see,' she said, clearly not seeing at all.

'A matter of business,' Catlin explained gently. 'I think.'

'I'll take your luggage up.' Conal's voice was totally without expression.

As he moved towards the staircase a small figure appeared at the top, looking down with intense interest.

'Oh!' it exclaimed. 'Oh, it's *you!*'

Catlin was not in the least surprised to see again the

small girl she had helped achieve her heart's desire that afternoon.

'Hello,' she responded, smiling with genuine warmth. 'I should have recognised you, Jenny. You have the Loring eyes.'

And that cool little air of self-command was a dead giveaway too. They all had it, all three of them, all watching her with those identical eyes.

Jenny smiled at her, but the wariness was clear for all to see. 'Mrs—Miss——' she broke off, scarlet, her confidence evaporating.

'You'd better call me Catlin. Anything else would sound a bit ridiculous, wouldn't it?'

Jenny looked for confirmation to her father. At his nod her colour subsided. 'Catlin helped me choose my new clothes this afternoon,' she told them in her clear precise little voice. 'Mrs Jansen hates them, but Catlin told her they're all the rage in Australia, so she let me buy them.'

'Just what are they?' Mrs Loring's question cracked like a whip while her hostile eyes were fixed on Catlin's vivid countenance as though she was offended by the glint of laughter in the warm golden eyes.

'We'll wait until later,' Conal interposed with enough of a command in his voice to make his mother stop glaring.

She nodded, saying stiffly, 'I've put Catherine in the blue bedroom.'

Conal looked at her. 'I said her old room,' he observed quite gently.

His mother drew in a sharp breath, but something in the hard blue glance stopped her from justifying herself. 'I must have misunderstood,' she said after a moment.

'It doesn't matter.' Catlin most emphatically did not want to go to her old bedroom. Part of the master suite, it was connected to Conal's rooms by a door to which, as she knew to her regret, there was no lock.

'Of course it doesn't,' he said smoothly now, 'but I think you'll be happier in your old room.'

He swung away up the stairs leaving an oddly frozen trio behind him. For a moment Emily Loring's feelings showed in a dreadful bitterness of expression before she turned away, leaving Jenny and Catlin alone together.

'I think I've forgotten the way,' Catlin said after a moment. 'Care to show me?'

'Yes, of course.' At the top of the stairs Jenny asked, 'How long are you going to stay, Cat—Catlin?'

'She doesn't know yet.' That was Conal, speaking through an open door, his glance warning Catlin not to contradict him.

She frowned but said nothing.

Jenny remarked, 'You have a funny name. Why does Gran call you Catherine?'

'Because my name is really the same as Catherine. Hundreds of years ago they were the same. Like Guinevere and Jennifer, and Jean and Jane.'

'Oh,' Jenny looked her interest. 'Are names really the same like that? What about Conal?'

'It's an Irish name,' her father told her. 'Your great-grandmother's maiden name, as a fact.' He laughed at his daughter's bewilderment and pinched her cheek. 'If you're really interested I'll explain it to you later. Now hop along and finish your homework. You may stay up and have dinner with us tonight as it's a special occasion.'

'Oh, *neat*!' Jenny flung her arms around her father's waist, hugging him hard. 'O.K., I'll do my homework, I promise. Afterwards will you play Battleships with me?'

'I might.'

As she watched the child dance off down the stairs Catlin's smile lingered. Whatever else had happened since she left, the past six years had only strengthened the bond between father and daughter.

'You look a little wistful,' he said, watching her.

'Wistful? No, I was just thinking it was nice.'

He looked at her with sardonic amusement. 'Revising your opinion of me?'

Conal had always been as sharp as a needle.

'Why should I? You always were pleasant to small children and old people, and no one could ever have doubted your love for Jenny.'

That amusement lingered in his hard gaze as he took her elbow and guided her into her room. 'Thank you for that testimonial, grudging though it was.'

He must have felt her instinctive, entirely involuntary withdrawal, the sharp flinching movement that jerked her arm away from his hand, but he said nothing and Catlin refused to look his way.

The room was almost exactly as it had been, the few pathetic belongings she had left behind still scattered about. Astonished, she lifted her brows, gazing around with interest and some dread. Had anything been needed to show her just how little those six months of her life meant to her now it was her reaction to this room where she had finally stopped being a child. A rather sentimental sympathy for that poor green girl who had wept her heart out in here, sobbing into the pillow so that the man next door wouldn't hear, that was all. Conal might not be prepared to let the past go, but she certainly was.

'Well, well,' she said, half smiling, relief lightening her voice so that it sounded almost gay. 'Are you in some kind of time warp here? I'd expected this room at least to be redecorated.'

He had put the case down on to a chair and was watching her, cold mockery glinting beneath the thick sweep of his lashes. 'Why?'

'Why not?' No way was she going to let him inside her brain. Or her heart, if it came to that.

He smiled. 'No necessity. As you should remember, I'm a careful man. Redecorating is expensive.'

Well, two could play at that game. 'Of course,' she said. 'How could I have forgotten?'

He wasn't, of course. He objected to waste, but he could be exceptionally generous. For the birthday she had had here he had given her a superb pair of chrysolite earrings, long antique drops of glittering golden stones, interspersed with diamonds, and for a moment made her feel that she had some future with him. Intuitively he had divined her aspirations exactly, the secret dreams of her heart and imagination. With those gems hanging elegantly against the smooth sweep of her neck she had had a vision of how she could be, given time and love and sophistication. Conal had been gentle with her that evening, almost tender, and her hopes had soared.

It hadn't lasted, of course. Only a month later she had found him with Belinda Scargill; the earrings had been left behind in her dash for freedom.

Wondering ruefully where they were now, she opened her suitcase and began to unpack.

'You travel light,' he remarked, apparently interested in this mundane chore.

Catlin cast him a sparkling look. 'Haven't you something else to do?'

'No.'

She shrugged, 'Well, it takes all sorts . . .' and began putting her clothes away, moving with precision and grace about the big room. Astonishingly she hadn't forgotten where things went; more astonishingly, everything was still there, her old clothes hung in the wardrobe and folded in the drawers of the armoire which leaned up against one wall.

'This is ridiculous,' she said tightly, extremely conscious of Conal sitting on the bed and watching her.

'What is?'

She flourished a skirt at him. 'Why wasn't this stuff got rid of, for heaven's sake?'

Broad shoulders lifted. 'At first we thought you'd come back. Then it seemed probable that you would send for your clothes. But you were determined to shake the dust entirely from your feet, weren't you, Catlin? Nothing that my money had bought went with you. I suppose after a time no one thought to do anything with these, so they were just left here.'

'Well, they can go,' she said, her expression hard as she began sweeping the rejected clothes into her suitcase. 'Most of them are totally unfashionable, but the material is still good. Someone will find a use for them.'

Conal shrugged and lay back on the bed, hands linked behind his head, watching her from beneath his lashes. 'Such a decisive lady,' he mused. 'Six years has made a big change, Catlin. What happened in them?'

'I told you—I grew up.' She spoke curtly, resenting his flagrant interest in her.

'So I see. How? What did you do after you left me?'

'Went to university.'

That black brow lifted. 'Indeed?'

'Yes.'

'And . . . ?'

She sighed ostentatiously, folding up a winter coat of tweed. 'Did an Accountancy degree, then worked for a big retail firm. Decided I preferred working with a smaller organisation, so I went to a firm of accountants in the suburbs. Which was where I met the owner of the shop I want to buy.'

'About which we will not talk.'

If Conal was surprised at her choice of career he gave no indication of it.

'For a week.' From her briefcase she took a folder and held it up. 'All the information is in here.'

'If I refuse to advance the money what will you do?'

She had thought it all out. 'Break the trust. I can— I'm over twenty and the only beneficiary.'

Not a muscle moved on the supine form on the bed. 'You could, if you *were* the only beneficiary. But you aren't. Your father in his wisdom made your unborn children beneficiaries too. And I'm sure I don't have to tell you that such a trust can't be broken.'

Catlin stared at him. After a moment she said with hard emphasis, 'I'd want to see that.'

'Your lawyer—John Stretton—knows.'

'Oh.' For a moment she stood irresolute, staring down at the garment in her hands, her brain working furiously behind the calm mask of her features. He would be correct; there was no reason for him to lie, but it wouldn't do any harm to check with Mr Stretton. And if this was true then it gave him a power over her until she could prove that there would be no further heirs. Suspicion stirred within her. From the corner of her eye she looked at him, saw the lean, angular features, the splendid body completely relaxed on her bed. He had taken off his coat and his fine shirt clung to his torso, emphasising his male attraction. The heavy lashes had drooped further so that she could not see what was going on in that clever remorseless brain.

With dry mouth she completed folding the dress into her suitcase. 'Then I'll have to go to court to vary the terms of the trust,' she said in a remote cold voice.

'In what way?'

'Either get rid of you on the grounds of conflicting interest or have at least one other trustee appointed.'

'You'd have some difficulty proving conflict of interest, as I'm sure Stretton would point out. Your investments have been kept strictly separate from my other affairs, and I've administered them well enough to double them.'

Resenting his cool judicial tone as he pointed this out, Catlin had to repress her temper.

'Perhaps so, but I'm sure I'll have no difficulty in proving that you're not exactly impartial where I'm concerned.'

The corners of the hard mouth lifted in a cynical smile. 'Oh, come now,' he drawled, opening his eyes to regard her with weary mockery. 'Are you insinuating that I'd let my personal feelings dictate my actions?'

'I'm insinuating nothing,' she said steadily, closing

the lid of her suitcase with great care so as not to slam it. 'Nothing at all. In any case, this conversation is singularly fruitless, as you haven't seen the figures or made a decision.'

'Of course.' That cool gaze moved from her face to her body, touching on breasts, waist and the length of her legs. It was a superbly insolent scrutiny shot through with a very masculine awareness of the symmetry of the form under the softly striped shirt and plain skirt of soft raw silk. Catlin's colour rose as she deliberately turned her back on him.

Much more of this, she thought grittily, and I'll have to recuperate from stress when I get back home. His dislike was only too obvious, as was his determination to make her jump to his tune. Witness this week, keeping her on tenterhooks, making it clear that if she didn't behave as he wanted her to any hope of getting the money was doomed.

Worth it, though, she told herself stoutly. Worth it to see the instantly hidden shock in both his and Emily's eyes when they had first seen her. That had gone a long way to easing old hurts. And when she went back to Australia with the purchase price of the shop and its stock she would think a week spent in his company a small price to pay.

After all, he would be at work during the day.

'You've matured very charmingly,' he said softly, surprising her by sitting up in a sudden movement. 'How old are you now?'

He knew, of course. 'Twenty-four. Which makes you—thirty-two, is it?'

'It is. Did you miss us when you'd gone, Catlin?'

What was this? She lifted her lashes, looked him full in the face. 'Yes. Just like a bad case of plague.'

'You hated us that much?'

Her throat was dry and harsh with remembered pain. 'One doesn't hate plague. One fears it and resents it and endures it and rejoices when it passes.'

'I see.' He got to his feet, moving with the litheness she remembered, and walked across the room to the intervening door. With his hand on the handle he told her brusquely, 'Dinner will be ready at seven-thirty. Do you want the bathroom now?'

'No, you use it first,' she said, suddenly exhausted.

The master suite had two main rooms. Between them was a small lobby where doors led to a bathroom and a dressing room which Conal used. The bathroom was big and compartmented, but Catlin felt uncomfortable about having to share it. No way, she thought grimly, no way was she going to run any risk of him coming in while she was showering or in a state of undress. During this week she would attend to her needs while he was at work.

For the moment she felt tired. The flight across the Tasman had been nothing, but the events of the subsequent hours had exhausted her. She hated living on a constant edge of tension, probing every word, listening to the silences, watching from beneath her lashes for the flicker of a muscle, the dark gleam in a glance, the small betrayals of body language, using them as signposts to guide her through the minefield that was life with Conal.

Yawning widely, she took off her skirt and shirt, pulling on a cotton wrap over her bra and pants. The bed looked inviting; it was made up, and she slipped between the sheets. Her room had once been the sitting room in the master suite. As a bedroom it had been furnished by Emily in a hurry under instructions from Conal immediately after their wedding. It was not one of Emily's better efforts. Striving for a degree of luxury, she had only managed to create a stuffy, over-opulent effect.

If her mother-in-law had wanted to intimidate the bashful seventeen-year-old her son had married she couldn't have chosen a better furnishing style. Catlin smiled sadly as her eye roamed from the superb antique armoire against one wall to the exquisite French chairs scattered around, the elegant chaise-longue and elaborate Roman blinds. She remembered, how clearly she remembered, her youthful unease in such sophisticated surroundings, her inability to move around without knocking into the furniture. A course at a modelling school had banished that gawkiness, greatly helped by her increasing self-confidence.

Quite suddenly she slept.

When she awoke it was almost dark. A quick glance at her watch revealed that she was going to have to move swiftly to make it downstairs in time for dinner. Fortunately, working had taught her how to get herself ready for the evening in a remarkably short time.

Half an hour later she was walking down the stairs, listening to the sound her elegant silk jacquard dress made against her legs as she moved. In a pale honey-beige, it was a soft blouson, its cut and style good, the only touches of drama one bare gold shoulder and the tasselled gold belt around her elasticised waist. Shoes the exact colour of the dress emphasised her height; she wore a plaited gold ring on her right hand and a spiral of gold in each ear. No wedding ring. She had left that behind when she fled.

It was on the ring that Emily Loring's gaze glittered when Catlin came into the parlour, as though it was a direct affront.

Jenny looked up from a book and smiled, mostly politeness, but with enough warmth to reveal a readiness to become friends. Her father was standing in the open French window, leaning against the jamb, both hands holding a drink, the sleek black head bowed slightly. He always looked fabulous, Catlin thought resentfully, even in jeans and the cotton shirts he wore when relaxing. Now, in a silk shirt and dark trousers, he had the faintly melancholy pride of a Spanish Grandee, lean and hawklike, the strong profile arrogant against the darkness outside.

At her appearance he turned his head. For a moment fire blazed in the depths of his eyes, immediately quenched by his thick lashes as he straightened up, saying blandly, 'Exactly on time, but you'd have been worth waiting for, Catlin.'

Would I indeed? she thought grimly, avoiding his gaze as she sat down on the sofa beside Jenny.

'What are you reading?' she asked.

Jenny sent a harried glance at her grandmother. *'The Little House in the Big Woods,'* she said softly, as though it was a sin to read in this house. 'By Laura Ingalls Wilder.'

Catlin nodded. 'Enjoying it?'

The child's expression lit up. 'I love it!' she breathed.

'How lucky you are! There are another five or six volumes to follow this one.'

'Truly?' Jenny looked dazzled at her good fortune.

'Truly.'

From behind them Emily commanded, 'Put your book away, Jenny. It's not polite to read when we have guests.'

Making sure that Catlin realised her position in this house, Catlin thought.

As Jenny obeyed, Conal asked his errant wife what she wanted to drink.

'White wine,' she told him. 'Dry if you have it, please.'

Mrs Loring looked down at her own glass of sherry. 'I believe it's very fashionable to drink white wine nowadays,' she remarked, making it sound like a solecism.

Faintly smiling, Catlin accepted a glass from Conal. 'It's the only alcohol that I can cope with. Everything else makes me sick or headachy.'

The sound of the doorbell stopped any further conversation on that subject. When Conal looked questioningly at his mother she said, 'Had you forgotten that the Perrotts were coming to dinner?'

'If you told me I must have,' he said.

That was all, but Catlin knew that Emily had not told him, that the Perrotts had probably been invited only after she knew of Catlin's arrival. And that Conal knew that too.

They were a pleasant couple, brother and sister; Lee and Angela, too courteous to give expression to their astonishment when Conal introduced her as his wife. Lee was a couple of years younger than his host, a couple of inches shorter, a little wider all round, like a good Rugby forward. Angela was lovely, with the kind of cool polished perfection seen only in those with time and money enough to spend a fortune on themselves. Smooth black hair drawn back from classical features, soft dark eyes above a red mouth, slender and graceful as a weeping willow. Not particularly bright, Catlin decided before the evening was halfway over but with looks and a manner like hers she didn't need brains. She worked in a travel agency and no doubt did her job superbly well.

And the fact that she hung on Conal's every word with the attention usually devoted only to demagogues and pop stars was no reason, Catlin told herself crisply, for being so catty. After all, six years ago she had given up any claim to him. The last thing she wanted was any kind of reconciliation. Peace, perhaps, a truce, but never again would she put herself in the position of being subordinate to him. That was what the whole object of her flight to Australia had been, to become self-aware, to discover herself before circumstances destroyed her real character forever. While she had lived with her father she had taken the place of the son he didn't have, and her personality had been stunted by the weight of his disappointment. Conal had further crushed her. It had taken her six years to rid herself of that feeling of worthlessness, and she was never again going to submit to it.

'How long are you here for?' Lee Perrott asked her, his eyes expressing his astonishment at her existence.

'We're not sure yet,' Conal interposed smoothly. 'More wine. Catlin?'

'No, thank you.'

And that was the end of that. For an hour or so, anyway, until Lee sat down beside Catlin while Angela and Conal were choosing a disc to put on the stereo.

'Hello, mystery lady,' he said softly, smiling, his regard just a little too bold. 'You know, you've knocked Angie into the most appalling loop. She had high hopes of becoming Mrs Conal Loring herself. We knew, of course, that there was an ex lurking around, but no one ever told us that she was a raving beauty, or that she wasn't an ex but very much in the picture. Tell me, where on earth have you been these last few years?'

Finding myself, Catlin could have said, but she didn't, merely telling him where she lived in an aloof voice that made him smile.

'And that's as far as I'm going to get,' he said, comprehending exactly. 'Fair enough. I see Conal looking this way with rather too much interest, so we'll discuss some nice uncontroversial subject. Tell me, do you think we'll be mining the asteroid belt within our lifetime? Bearing in mind the fact that I personally intend living to one hundred and twenty?'

Catlin laughed, as he intended her to, then surprised him by giving a reasoned answer to his question. It only took her a few minutes to discover that beneath the rather brash exterior there was a good brain. They argued amiably for a while on the advantages of space exploration until Angela drifted back across the room and said in a weary tone, 'Lee, you must be boring Catherine to screaming point—not to mention others. Why not talk about something relevant?'

'The name,' Catlin said deliberately, 'is Catlin. C-a-t-l-i-n. It's a Middle English version of Catherine, but as Catlin it's an old family name and that's what people call me. If they want me to answer.'

There was a dreadful little silence. Angela flushed,

suddenly young and vulnerable, and looked around for help. 'I thought——' she said breathlessly, 'at least, I'm sure that Mrs Loring called you Catherine. I'm sorry.'

Like hitting a baby, Catlin decided gloomily, wondering just what there was about the younger woman that made her want to give her a good kick.

'She does,' she agreed cheerfully, 'but she's the only one. I'm quite used to repeating my name, it's so unusual that most people do a double-take when I'm introduced. Once it's explained they remember me, even if it's only as the woman with the weird name.'

Angela nodded, her composure restored, but Lee murmured softly, 'That's not why I'd remember you,' and from behind the sofa Conal, his hands on her shoulders, said with calm insolence, 'It's appropriate, don't you think? That mane of tawny hair and the lithe graceful movements—definitely feline.'

No doubt he was referring to her behaviour too. Catlin leaned back and smiled up into his face; inverted, the strong bones and lines were emphasised into harshness.

'Then I should be Leona or Leonie,' she said, angered by his deliberate touch. Against the skin of her bare shoulder his fingers were lean and very strong; they moved slowly across the fine bones, stamping her with the mark of his possession. His touch was hateful to her, but she could not make any outcry and he knew it.

Lee and Angela too were watching that possessive hand. Lee's eyes were bright with interest, but his sister looked away, swallowing fiercely as though the sight was agony to her.

'Or Leontyne,' said Conal with eyes only for his wife, his glance glittering with malice as it raked her face.

'Oh—Conal?' That was Emily from across the room, her normally smooth voice uneven. 'Darling, a cricket has just got in. Do you think you could——?'

Conal could, and did, pulling the screens across to the accompaniment of pleas from Angela not to kill it, and the incident was closed. It left a nasty taste in Catlin's mouth.

CHAPTER THREE

'I THINK we'd better have a talk,' Catlin said abruptly as they walked up the stairs together.

'Your room or mine?'

Her teeth clamped on to her lip. No way was she going into his room, and Emily had successfully circumvented any chance of a private talk by making it quite clear that she was prepared to stay up all night rather than leave them alone together.

'How about the study?' she said.

Conal looked at her with cold sarcasm. 'I'm on my way to bed.'

'Oh, my room, I suppose.' As she opened the door she added. 'Now.'

'You're pushing your luck, Catlin. Nobody gives me orders.'

Catlin looked at him, her glance level and accusing.

'Me neither,' she said quietly. 'And nobody, *nobody* mauls me without my permission. I don't know what game you were playing down there and I don't want to know, but I'll have no part of it, Conal. If you don't leave me alone I'll go back to the hotel.'

He had been watching her, his expression unreadable, the dark skin tightened over his cheekbones and his mouth a firm straight line. Now he said indifferently, 'I'm your husband. I have the right to touch you.'

'That idea is long out of date,' she retorted scornfully. 'You have nothing! No man has any rights unless I grant them, and I made it quite clear how I felt about your rights when I left you six years ago.'

'So you did—very publicly.'

She shrugged. 'At the time I wasn't thinking too straight, but I doubt whether we'd have been able to

come to any more amicable arrangement. After——'
She stopped precipitately. Her tongue touched her lip
before she finished, 'after what happened.'

As if her reticence angered him he thrust his hands
into his pockets and walked over to the window. Over
his shoulder he said calmly, 'I suppose that now is as
good a time as any to tell you that I'm sorry for my
behaviour before you left. The only extenuating
circumstance I can plead is that I was just as unhappy
about things as you and there seemed nothing I could
do about it. I hadn't intended to hurt you, ever, and yet
you were being hurt more and more each day that
passed.'

He took his hands from his pockets and straightened
up, turning to face her. The hooded gaze rested on her
face. There was a chill watchfulness in his stance that
made her skin prickle in unease.

'You were so defenceless it made me angry,' he
continued after a moment. 'When you came in that
night and began shouting at me I lost control
completely. Nothing I can say can make up for what I
did, but if it's any consolation, when you ran away I
went almost out of my mind.'

A figure of speech, of course. There was simply no
way she could imagine Conal worrying enough about
anyone, except perhaps Jenny, to be as upset as that.
Still, he had apologised. Not for sleeping with Belinda
What's-her-name, or making his wife's life a living hell
before that, but one couldn't expect everything.

How civilised we are, she thought on a spurt of bitter
amusement. No reference to rape, nothing heavy! Polite
evasions, a smooth apology and she, no doubt, was
expected to be suitably grateful.

'Catlin?'

'It's six years ago,' she said without emotion. 'If you
want my forgiveness then you have it. I no longer care
very much.'

'Yet you can't bear to have me touch you.'

A pause. Catlin stood rigidly immobile, one hand clenched at her side. Suavely he continued, 'It is just me, I presume. Or do you stiffen and flinch when any man touches you?'

'That's none of your business.'

'We're not divorced.'

A frown drew her brows together. Warily she shot a swift glance in his direction, met the cold impassivity of his expression with a certain bewilderment, hastily hidden. What the hell was he up to now? Summoning up a stiff hauteur she had found useful in the past she stressed, 'I don't consider that we were ever married.'

'Legally we are—signed, sealed and consummated. Why didn't you divorce me, Cat?'

Wariness crawled across her skin. She shrugged. 'Living in Australia made things awkward. Anyway, *I* left *you*. At that time you would have had to divorce me for desertion, I had no grounds except mental cruelty.'

'Or adultery.'

She turned away, picked up her hairbrush from the dressing table and agreed tonelessly, 'Yes, of course.' And before he could ask her why she hadn't made use of that, she asked, 'Why didn't you divorce me?'

'It wasn't necessary. I didn't feel any need to marry again.'

'Poor Angela,' she said sweetly. 'Don't you think you should tell her that? Emily, too. She seems to think you need a wife, if her behaviour tonight gave any indication of her feelings. Tell me, does she still not know of your amorous activities—outside wedlock, that is?'

Fear kicked her in the pit of her stomach. Moving with the lithe grace she had once so admired, Conal came across to stand in front of her, his features hard as a bronze mask. 'I certainly don't discuss my amours with her,' he said softly, taking the brush from between her nerveless fingers, 'but I imagine she's been enlightened. There's always someone only too eager to hand on juicy titbits of gossip in the hope that they'll hurt.'

'Oh, *always*!' she returned savagely, while memories darkened the vivid gold of her eyes to dullness.

He was too close, deliberately looming over her, his broad shoulders blocking the light from the one glowing lamp in the room. She could hear the soft sound of his breathing, even catch a faint taunting hint of his masculine scent, clean and slightly salty. And with it he exuded menace, cold and controlled.

If she shrank back he would know just how thin her composure was, so she stood defiantly facing him. He looked down at the hairbrush and reached beyond her, just brushing her hip, to put it back on the dressing table. His touch tormented, but she lifted a cold, proud face, determined not to show any emotion. This was the kind of cat and mouse game he enjoyed, designed to reduce her to a trembling wreck. Never again would she give him the satisfaction of knowing just how well he succeeded.

He smiled, teeth very white in the darkness of his face, his eyes half closed as he watched her. Slowly, without any hurry, he lifted his hand and touched the spiral of gold in her ear. The warmth of his fingers against her skin brought the blood drumming to her pulses, but beyond a dilation of her pupils she made no movement.

The earrings fastened by means of a hook. Working with tantalising slowness, Conal took one out and then the other, using the opportunity to apply the most subtle of caresses, stopping finally with his finger over the betraying little beat beneath her ear.

'Afraid of me, Cat?'

Oh, yes, and furiously, icily angry; too afraid to give rein to her anger. He was still smiling, but she could sense other, darker feelings waiting beneath the veneer of his amusement.

Battening down her emotions, she lifted her lashes to reveal eyes as limpid and calm as a mountain pool, the wildness his touch had roused completely banished.

'Don't I have reason?' she asked gently.

His gaze narrowed as it swept her face, fiercely trying to penetrate the silken skin and strong, lovely bone structure. She sensed rather than saw his bafflement and inwardly rejoiced with the cold, clear exhilaration of victory. His attempt to rouse her physically had succeeded but he didn't realise it.

Now she knew that she was a match for him. No longer like an open book, all of her juvenile emotions spread out on display. He was unable now to read her with insulting ease and despise her for her naïvety.

'Perhaps,' he said after several moments of intense scrutiny. His glance dropped, as did his hand; his fingers made a loose shackle about her wrist. 'You misunderstood what I said. I don't want to marry again, but I do need a wife, if only to give Jenny the same sort of home life as her friends. Mama has coped very well up until now, but this last year she has not been particularly well. Running around after Jenny exhausts her. I think she dreads having to guide another adolescent through those turbulent years.'

Catlin's eyes flew open. He smiled smoothly. 'I gave her a hard time.'

She drew a deep breath. 'You?' Her glance was golden with sarcasm. 'Never! Why, she's told me a hundred times how perfect you are, were, and always will be.'

The light clasp on her wrist tightened. 'A common enough illusion among devoted mothers,' he said dryly. 'Pertness doesn't suit you, Cat.'

His casual, insolent shortening of her name infuriated her, a fact of which was well aware. So did the deliberate put-down tone of an adult speaking to a cheeky child. 'How glad I am that I don't have to worry about your opinions any more,' she shot back, speaking between her teeth as she tried to jerk her wrist free.

It was a stupid thing to do. He laughed and bent his head and kissed her, holding her head between cruel hands as he took advantage of her stunned astonishment to force her mouth open in a trespass which was as blatant as it was unforgivable.

When it ended she was shaking and white-faced, the back of her hand pressed to her bruised mouth as she fought to control her reaction. When she had first lived in Australia she had joined a class in self-defence; she was more than capable of defending herself, but the shock of his mouth on hers had driven every precept from her mind.

'Don't look at me like that!' he exclaimed harshly. 'For Pete's sake, Catlin, it was a kiss—nothing more.'

Shivering, her skin cold and damp, she swallowed, then swallowed again, closing her eyes against the shocked astonishment of his expression.

When she spoke she had to force the words past her dry throat. They sounded croaky, as though he had tried to strangle her.

'I'm going,' she said, and then, more strongly, 'I must go.'

'No!' Conal caught her shoulders, forcing her to stand still. Like her he was pale, tanned skin stretched tight over suddenly prominent bones. 'Is that what I did to you?' he demanded. 'Can you not bear a man to touch you?'

By now her courage was coming back. A bitter kind of pride forced her chin in the air. 'Only you,' she said, each word cold and clear. 'Other men don't worry me in the least.'

'I—see.' Slowly he released her, turning away so that she could only see the beautiful line of his profile. Somewhere deep within her a faint pull of emotion made itself felt. He was looking shattered.

Good, she thought fiercely, whipping up her anger

afresh. Serves him right! Her instinctive revulsion, for that must be what it was, had hit him right where it hurt, in his sexual pride.

'And have there been others?'

For a moment she hesitated before lying, 'What do you think? When I left you I was a mess, my self-confidence gone. I had this weird idea that I had to prove myself—I went to university to convince myself that I wasn't stupid; I learned how to cook and how to run a house and be a good hostess, I even took part in the sports you considered so important, sailing and swimming and flying. It seemed important to me to show you. Like the child you called me, I suppose. You seemed to prefer experienced women, so I became experienced.' She laughed, her clear voice cynical. 'Fortunately, after a couple of years, I came to my senses and realised that no man was worth promiscuity. I'm a lot more discriminating now.'

Silence stretched between them, almost tangible, heavy with the weight of her words. Conal had thrust his hands back into his pockets and, white around the thin line of his mouth, was staring at the carpet.

Catlin pressed home the point. 'So if you want to divorce me for infidelity you'd be able to. However, I can promise not to embarrass you or Emily while I'm here. Like you, I don't go in for one-night stands.'

His head jerked towards her. 'Have you a lover now?' he asked thinly.

Again she hesitated, and again she lied.

'Yes,' she said, and watched with pleasure as his expression hardened into stone. 'Not that it's any of your business.'

'So you keep saying.' He walked across to the door which separated their rooms as though her confession had so disgusted him that he couldn't bear the sight of her any longer. But when his fingers touched the handle he said deliberately, 'You surprise me. I'd have thought you had more strength of character than to lose your grip so completely. And let's get one thing straight, shall we, before we forget the whole incident. You fought like the devil that night, but you wanted me just as much as I wanted you. You provoked my onslaught with your taunts—you had a vicious tongue, even then.'

'Typical!' she sneered. 'I had every reason to be angry! Or do you think I should have accepted your mistress as my best friend? You didn't rape me because you wanted to take me to bed, you did it because you were furious and it made you feel good to use your strength to subdue me. It was either rape me or beat me, and by then you knew me well enough to realise which would humiliate me the most!'

Conal turned, his mouth moving in that fixed, humourless smile. 'It did indeed,' he said softly, stripping her with his eyes so that she felt aflame with embarrassment and shame. 'Make me feel good, I mean. As for the other—yes, I'll admit to being savagely angry with you, but I wanted you. And like it or not, admit it or not, you wanted me. When I first touched you you were already aroused; by the time we ended up on my bed you were wild for me. Your own desires betrayed you. That's why you loathe my touch, because you're afraid of the response of your body. Last time it blew your mind.'

'And then you hurt me.'

He shrugged at the bitter accusation in her voice. 'There was nothing I could have done about that.'

'You could have been more gentle,' she flashed fiercely.

'Perhaps. I certainly wasn't thinking straight. If I'd realised—but, hell, you blew my mind too! I married a schoolgirl; I certainly didn't expect to find a tigress in my bed.' He watched as Catlin pressed her hands to her hot cheeks, adding in slightly more gentle tones, 'It would still have hurt like hell, Cat. You just happened to be one of the unfortunate ones, as I'm sure you know now. I'd assumed that because you'd spent most of your time on horseback the first time would be easy for you. I was mistaken. It didn't hurt the second time, did it?'

By now her colour had ebbed. Shocked though she was by his casual admission that he had thought of making love to her before that traumatic occasion, she pushed this knowledge to the back of her mind as she grappled with the implications of his question. What else could she say but no! As usual he was right; she knew now, as she hadn't when a naïve eighteen years old, that some, a few, women found the initial act of love painful. As Conal said, she was one of the unfortunate ones.

'So why continue to blame me for something that was inevitable?' he asked coldly. 'I'm sorry your initiation was so disappointing. I suppose every woman would like to feel sentimental about her first lover and I've deprived you of that. However, you should have stored up plenty of infinitely more pleasant memories to help you forget my barbaric embraces.'

There it was again, the manoeuvring of her into a position where she was the one who felt guilty and stupid for being affected by his actions! A little more of her confidence crumbled, but she refused to allow herself to be manipulated.

'Plenty,' she said calmly, forcing a small and, she hoped, reminiscent smile to her lips. 'So you feel that everything that happened was my fault? Clearly I had no right to be resentful of the fact that you and Belinda What's-her-name were lovers, certainly no reason to quarrel with you, and should never have resented the fact that you raped me? Because you did, Conal. I might have been aroused, but I didn't want to make love with you and you forced me. As far as I'm concerned that's rape.'

'I agree.' He opened the door into his room and stood, dark against the darkness beyond, his expression aloof and bored. 'And I've apologised. I don't feel proud of myself for that episode. Now that I've seen how it's affected you—your reaction to my touch is pretty extreme—I feel even less proud. But I refuse to shoulder the entire blame. Perhaps when you admit to yourself just why you goaded me into forcing you that night you'll be free.'

'I am free.'

In the dimness his expression was unfathomable, but there was a deep sardonic note in his voice which made her clutch her anger.

'Free? You're so aware of me, so keyed up whenever we're in the same room——'

'Shut up!' Caution forgotten, Catlin spat the words out, even taking several steps towards him, one hand lifting to slap the mocking smile from his face.

'Don't be stupid.' The bored instruction stopped her instantly. 'Calm down, Cat. You hate my guts, but we have unfinished business, you and I, and you're staying here until it's completed.'

'I'm leaving tomorrow.'

'Do that and you can kiss your money goodbye.' As she opened her mouth to speak Conal strolled back into the room and caught her chin, holding it up so that he could see her flushed, infuriated face. 'Oh, you could probably have me deposed as a trustee, but it will take time and you'll lose your chance with that particular business. Just be a good girl and do as you're told, and if your figures are anywhere near respectable you'll have your bookshop.'

'Don't be so bloody patronising,' she jerked from between clenched teeth. 'I'm twenty-four years old now, Conal, not eighteen and blinded by my first infatuation.'

'No, you're not, but you've never really got over it, have you.' He stared down into her mutinous face, at the wilful lips curbed into a straight hard line, great gold-brown eyes flaming with anger, and he smiled with a rather bitter irony. 'Just call on some self-control, my dear,' he said, and traced the outline of her lips with a lean brown finger.

Her lashes drooped. Resisting with immense difficulty the impulse to bite him, she wrenched her chin from his hold and stepped back, saying coldly, 'As I have no alternative, I'll stay. But I meant what I said. I'm going to have you deposed as quickly as I can. There's no way I'm going to put up with your bullying whenever I want some money.'

The hooded gaze was watchful. 'Why don't you live on it? Your income is big enough for you to have a much easier life than one behind the counter in a bookshop. Or in an accountant's office.'

'Because I'd die of boredom.' She looked at him with smouldering resentment but the self-restraint she had worked so hard to achieve was once more within her reach and her voice was as cold as his, as indifferent. 'I had six months of that life, Conal, remember? It nearly drove me out of my head.'

'So you gained one thing from being my wife.' He smiled and said, 'Goodnight, Cat. I'll see you in the morning.'

It took her over an hour to get to sleep and almost immediately it seemed she was woken by someone banging on the door. Yawning, confused, she switched on the lamp at her bedside, trying to peer at her watch with eyes that were extremely reluctant to open.

Three-thirty-five!

'Coming!' she called, scrambling out of bed, but Conal was already halfway across the room.

'Something's wrong with Mama,' he told her harshly as she struggled into her dressing gown. 'I've called the doctor and he and the ambulance are on the way, but Jenny's awake and upset. Can you comfort her?'

'Of course, Conal. What——?'

'I don't know.'

She nodded, going before him through the door. As

she turned towards Jenny's room he said bleakly, 'It could be a stroke.'

'Oh.' She said nothing more, but her hand grasped his in the age-old gesture of comfort. For a moment he hesitated, then returned the pressure before making his way swiftly to Emily's room.

Jenny was tearful, her blue eyes enormous in her pale little face. 'I heard a noise,' she sobbed forlornly. 'A horrible noise. Catlin, what's happened?'

'It's all right, darling.' Catlin dropped on to the side of the bed, holding the thin hands in a warm comforting clasp. 'Gran is ill, but Daddy has everything under control. The doctor is on his way.'

Fear receded, but Jenny whispered, 'Will she—is she going to *die*?'

'I don't see why.' Catlin longed to draw the child close to her, but such a gesture would be premature. 'She's a pretty tough lady, your gran, just like you and Daddy. I can't see her dying yet awhile.'

Even as the soft childish mouth moved in a small smile tears sprang again into Jenny's eyes. 'I was mad with her tonight,' she whispered frantically. 'I wanted her to go away and leave me alone.'

'And I suppose she was cross with you, too,' said Catlin, her tender heart aching for the terrors of childhood. 'But nothing has happened to you, has it?'

The dark head moved in negation.

'And think of all the other times you've been angry with her and nothing has happened. Everyone gets angry with the people they love sometimes—that's life. Just because you were mad with Gran tonight it doesn't mean that you've made her ill.'

Silence while Jenny digested this. After a moment she nodded. 'I was just being a bit silly, I s'pose,' she admitted shyly. 'Will you stay with me?'

'Until you go to sleep, yes.'

Catlin switched off the main lamp leaving only the soft small glimmer of the night light. Jenny cuddled back against the pillow, one hand clasping Catlin's, but although she lay quietly with lashes lowered, she did not go back to sleep. Like Catlin, she was listening.

Within a few minutes the doctor arrived; only a short time after that the intermittent flash of a red light coming up the drive heralded the ambulance.

'Catlin?'

'Yes, darling?'

'Are you sure she's going to get better?'

Catlin bit her lip but told the truth. 'No, but I'm pretty sure. As I said, she's a tough bird, your gran. She doesn't want to die, and that's more than half the battle.'

Within a few seconds there came a soft tap at the door. 'That will be Daddy,' Catlin said softly. 'Lie still while I talk to him, will you?'

Conal looked older, the fine skin drawn sharply over the bones of his face. 'It appears to be a stroke,' he said curtly. 'At first glance, not a severe one, but she'll be in hospital for some time. I'll go in with her now. Do you mind staying with Jenny?'

'Not in the least.'

Her prompt reply eased some of the tension in his expression. 'Good girl,' he said, then kissed Jenny before walking down the corridor.

Catlin watched him go, striding with the superb carriage of an athlete, smooth, fast-moving, possessed of a kind of masculine grace which enchanted the eye.

Jenny's voice recalled her to herself. Cutting short a sigh, she turned and went back into her stepdaughter's room.

Half an hour later she said wearily, 'Listen, love, why don't you come and spend the rest of the night with me? I've got a great big bed, plenty of room for two. And we'll leave the door between Daddy's and my room open so that if he rings up we'll hear it easily.'

This suggestion met with such eager approval that Catlin felt a warning pang deep in her heart. It would be cruel to allow Jenny to become fond of her when she planned to be here for such a short time. But tonight—well, the child needed reassurance badly.

Once they were in the bed Jenny said dreamily, 'On a Sunday morning sometimes Daddy lets me climb into his bed. You smell nice, Catlin.'

'So do you.'

A swift giggle, then the child turned away, snuggling her back against Catlin. 'You feel nice, too.'

'Goodnight, darling.'

'Goodnight.'

In spite of her concern for Emily Catlin slept almost instantly, but her sleep was troubled by dreams, and it was with heavy eyes that she woke, her head and neck aching and her mouth dry.

Beside her Jenny still slept, cuddled close, her rounded brown cheek resting on Catlin's arm, her body relaxed in the innocent abandon of childhood.

From behind Catlin's shoulder came her husband's voice, dry, faintly sarcastic. 'Strange bedfellows! Do you realise that it's almost eight o'clock?'

Without disturbing the child Catlin turned her head. He was standing by the window, a mug of coffee in his hand, fully dressed in a dark business suit.

'How is she?'

He drained the coffee, setting the mug down on the windowsill. 'She'll pull through. It was a slight stroke.'

'Good.' Catlin looked back at the child nestling so confidingly against her. 'I hope this hasn't broken one of your domestic commandments. She couldn't get back to sleep by herself.'

The blue gaze mocked her. 'You look very sweet. Hard to tell which is the child when both faces are serene in sleep. No, our domestic commandments don't forbid finding comfort in whatever way we can. But it's time for her to wake. I'll drop her off at school on my way to work.'

'Oh, but surely she can stay——'

Her instinctive protest was overborne. 'Now that *is* a domestic commandment. Nothing, but nothing, interferes with school. She'll be better for having something to occupy her mind.'

Which was probably true, but couldn't he understand that for a child of Jenny's age it must be shattering to see the only mother she had ever known borne off to hospital?

After a moment she said, 'Oh, you're hard!'

His narrowed glance swept across her face and shoulders, bare beneath the thin straps of her nightdress. 'You're surprised?'

'No,' she snapped. 'O.K., if you'll get out of here I'll get her up.'

His soft taunting laughter rang in her ears even after he had left. Catlin waited a moment until the flush on her cheeks and throat had subsided before giving Jenny a gentle shake.

She woke sweetly and swiftly, kissing Catlin on the cheek before running into her father's room. While Catlin dressed she heard the high voice prattling next door, but by the time she locked herself into the bathroom Jenny had gone.

As the housekeeper did not live in and didn't arrive until eight-thirty it was left to Catlin to prepare breakfast, which she did with only a few delays because of the strange kitchen. Jenny ate a boiled egg and some fruit and toast. Completely reassured by her father's conviction that all was well with Emily, she chatted brightly, telling Catlin of a trip her class was to take that day. Apparently Conal had made his own meal, for he poured himself another cup of coffee, refusing Catlin's offer of food. If he had eaten he had cleared up behind him. The kitchen was immaculate but beginning to show its age. It could, Catlin decided over her pineapple slices, do with a complete redecoration and restructuring to make things easier for whoever did the cooking.

Conal's voice broke into her reverie, faintly acid. 'No doubt you can drive?'

'Yes.' Only she knew how much pleasure her answer gave her. Her lack of confidence on Auckland's roads had been the cause of many of Emily's cutting comments.

'Then you'd better read up the differences between our road code and the one you're used to. There's a copy of it in the bookcase in my study. Public transport is not particularly convenient out here and when Mama is well enough to have visitors Jenny will want to go and see her.'

'Yes, please.' For a moment a shadow darkened his daughter's eyes, but it was soon gone. 'How long will she be in hospital, Daddy?'

'I don't know. Some weeks, I'm afraid.' As he spoke he looked at Catlin, his gaze holding hers for a long moment. Then he smiled down at his daughter. 'Today you're going rock-pooling, I believe.'

While Jenny told him in quick, eager tones about her class trip Catlin drank coffee, her face impassive as she pondered the significance of that long assessing glance.

When Mrs Jansen arrived the expression of her astonishment and forebodings took some time and required a cup of tea to accompany her.

'Poor thing,' the housekeeper ended comfortably. 'But as long as she's not paralysed or anything.'

'Well, Conal didn't say she was and he certainly didn't seem to be worried.'

'Not to say that he's not,' said Mrs Jansen with a conspiratorial smile. 'If he doesn't want to show anything there's precious little to see in his face, is there? He doesn't wear his feelings on his sleeve.'

Catlin nodded, keeping her own face without expression. 'You're right, but I think he'd have told me in this case.'

'Well, I'm glad. At least she'll be able to rest. She's been overdoing things, you know, and young Jenny really keeps her on her toes, rushing here and rushing there. Mrs Loring is determined that she's not going to miss out on anything just because she hasn't got a mother, so she ferries her around after school taking her to dancing and skating and Pony Club. It's just getting too much for her.'

Catlin nodded but said nothing, oddly irritated by this different view of Emily's character.

After a moment Mrs Jansen went on, 'I'm not usually so indiscreet, but—well, I suppose it's all in the family, isn't it?'

Once more Catlin nodded, aware that there was no way she could satisfy Mrs Jansen's curiosity.

'Well, I'd better get to work, I suppose,' the older woman said briskly, setting her cup down. 'You will give her my best wishes for her quick recovery when you go to see her, won't you?'

'Yes, of course.' Catlin made a mental note to tell Conal, not feeling it necessary to explain that it was highly unlikely that she would be visiting Emily. Not if she wanted to allow her to recover quickly, anyway.

The day passed oddly pleasantly. Catlin worked with Mrs Jansen, finding enjoyment in the age-old tasks of polishing and tidying and cleaning.

After lunch she was sleepy and curled up in a hammock between two jacaranda trees, watching with heavy eyelids the soft patterns made by the interlacing leaf fronds until she slept.

When she woke Jenny was lying on the ground beneath her, nose in a book, her thin legs stretched out behind, chin resting on her hands.

'Oh dear!' Catlin yawned, feeling like death.

'Mrs Jansen said you probably still had jet-lag and not to wake you. I brought you an orange drink with ice cubes in it. It's melted, but there's still some bits of ice in it if you want it. Catlin, what's jet-lag?'

By the time Catlin had attempted an explanation which eventually ended up in a darkened room with a candle and a watermelon to explain the mystery of time zones it was almost five.

'Well, I think I see what you mean,' Jenny said politely, adding, 'At least I know now why it's dark in England when it's daytime here. Catlin, would you like to have a swim?'

'Love one!'

'Pool or beach?'

Catlin smiled. 'Let's try the sea, shall we? Have you any homework?'

'Only a little, but I'm so hot and sticky.'

'O.K., sweetie.' Fortunately she had packed a bathing suit, a maillot in black which was so light that its existence was barely felt.

Mrs Jansen, waiting downstairs, said with a laughing rueful glance at her own comfortable curves, 'What it is to be young and long-legged and slim! I'll be going now, Mrs Loring.' She paused before continuing, 'My daughter Karen babysits for young Jenny. If you want to use her she'll be available. She's doing Scholarship this year, so she brings her books along and swots.'

'Thank you.' Catlin looked through the door to where Jenny capered on the lawn. 'I don't suppose we'll be needing a babysitter, but be sure that if we do I'll keep Karen in mind.'

'Good. Well, I'll see you tomorrow.'

The sea was cold, much colder than Catlin was accustomed to, but it was refreshing too. After the initial shock she revelled in it, swimming races with Jenny up and down the little cove. Above them the pohutukawas clung to the cliff-face, and wherever the sun could reach the ground great clumps of agapanthus held blue and white puffballs of bloom to the sky. The sea shimmered gold and silver against the dark bulk of Rangitoto.

'What does Rangitoto mean?' Jenny demanded.

'Island of the Bleeding Sky. At least that's what some people say, because it was a volcano. But I have heard others give it a much longer name which means "The Days of the Bleeding of Tama-te-kapua" because a famous chief of the Arawa Canoe was badly wounded there.'

'Which one is right?'

Catlin laughed. This childhood passion for things to be right or wrong, black or white, with no puzzling, worrying shades of grey in between! 'I don't know, Jenny.'

'Oh. Catlin, why do the Maoris talk about being descended from a Canoe? You said that chief who was hurt was of the Arawa Canoe. Why?'

'Because, like us, the Maori people came here as settlers. But they came long before us and they came in canoes, all of which had names. All the people in one canoe were usually related to each other and they settled together. Because they were proud of the fact that they'd made such a long hard voyage and because they are a race of great orators, great poets, they described themselves as the children of that canoe.'

The black head nodded thoughtfully. 'Are you going to stay with us now, Catlin? Have you come back here to live?'

They were sitting side by side just where the water met the sand, small waves creaming up their legs to meet around the back. Catlin looked down at Jenny's sleek dark head, smooth as a seal's, and said slowly, 'No, I haven't. As I told you in the shop, I'm here on business. When that's finished I'll go back to Australia.'

'I wish you didn't have to,' Jenny said wistfully, staring straight out to sea. 'I like having you here.'

And just how did one answer that? Truthfully and feel an utter heel, or with comfortable lies?

Before Catlin had worked out what to say Conal spoke from behind them, his cool voice tinged with cynicism.

'Don't get too upset, Jenny darling. If we ask her politely I'm sure Catlin will stay with us at least until Gran comes out of hospital.'

CHAPTER FOUR

IT WAS just as well that the long years had taught her self-control. After the first searing, contemptuous glance she had avoided looking directly at him, taking care to lift her eyes no higher than his beautiful, chiselled mouth.

And when Jenny had gone to bed she said with cold distaste, 'That was unforgivable.'

The broad shoulders moved in a slight shrug. 'You've forgiven worse things.'

This time she forced herself to meet the hard irony of his gaze. 'You should have realised by now how much I hate being forced,' she said harshly. 'I can see that it gives you a kind of sick enjoyment to pull strings and watch your puppet dance, but this is the last time, I promise you. Once I get back to Australia I'm never going to be put in a position where you have any power over me or my affairs.'

'Brave words, bravely spoken!' The mockery scorched along her nerve-ends, bringing her yellow-amber head up in an indignant movement, great eyes glittering with rage.

He laughed and reached out a hand, running an insolent finger from cheek to ear. Catlin jerked her head away, but he caught a handful of her hair and held her to the wall, his hand splayed across the soft tresses, the knuckle hard against her cheekbone.

'Don't move,' he said coolly, watching her from beneath drooping lashes. His other hand came up and began to touch her ear, the long sensitive fingers exploring the intricate convolutions with a sensuality that drove the breath from Catlin's lungs.

Rage mixed with terror whitened her face.

'I'm not going to hurt you,' he said with soft emphasis, speaking soothingly like a man trying to calm a panic-stricken animal. 'It's all right, Cat. You have to get over this. Don't you see, while you're so frightened of me you'll always be in my power.'

His hand moved slowly from her ear to her throat, finding pleasure in the long silken sweep of it. The cruel grip on her hair eased, he looked gravely into her wide eyes, holding her still by sheer force of will as long fingers stroked the vulnerable nape of her neck.

'Relax,' he said softly, his hooded gaze enigmatic. 'I won't hurt you—or try to get you into bed. You look like a goat pegged out for a tiger—terrified!'

'Does it flick your ego to know that I find your touch unbearable?' Her voice was hoarse and painful.

He smiled suddenly, but there was little amusement in the depths of his eyes. 'Strikes at my pride,' he admitted.

'So this is sheer conceit.' If she kept talking she could concentrate on her words, not on the way his fingers moved across her skin with tantalising gentleness as though he found her woman's body incredibly beautiful.

'Not entirely. I meant what I said. You will never be free of me if I terrify you into losing your wits as I do now. There are different kinds of bondage, you know. Great love is one kind, physical fear another.'

'How about the remembrance of past humiliation?'

Anger glittered in the depths of his eyes, but the slow, remorseless caressing continued, as though his hands possessed a life of their own. Catlin closed her eyes, trying fiercely to summon up the maxims her self-defence class had taught her. Gently, so lightly that she couldn't understand why every touch seemed burned into her skin, he shaped her face, running his fingers along the strong line of her jaw, the high cheekbone, winging across her brows. The blood surged back into her face while her heart beat loudly in her ears.

'Is that how you remember it?' Conal said quietly. 'I admit I intended humiliation at first, but it didn't take long for that to go by the board. Angry though we both were, you must have realised that.'

'You hated me.'

'No!' Slowly but inexorably he drew her close, holding her rigid body loosely. His cheek came down on her forehead. 'No, never,' he said when she froze, her breath stilling in her throat. 'How could I hate you? You were bitterly unhappy, and it was my fault. Oh, I was angry, probably angrier than I've ever been before or since, but that was because I was in the wrong. Instead of sitting down and trying to work things out like reasonable human beings we both lost our tempers and heaven knows, said and did some cruel things.'

She flinched, pulling away, but he refused to let her go. Panic sparked along her veins, she whispered, 'Please—oh, please!' her voice thin with fear.

'I won't hurt you. Relax, Catlin, just let yourself go limp. Are you sure that it's me you're frightened of and not yourself?'

She was suddenly still. 'What do you mean?'

'Just that what humiliates you so when you remember the night we made love is not my rape but your response to it.'

Crack! Ashen-faced Catlin stared at him with hatred dark and consuming in her eyes.

He laughed, taunting, 'Did I get too close to the truth then, darling?'

'No!' she spat fiercely, both hands clenched at her sides. The one she had hit him with smarted, for she had caught him over the cheekbone, but it was nothing compared to the pain in her heart. For a moment, just a moment, she had let him get to her. He had sounded sincere, but she should have known that he had been baiting a trap for her.

She had thought herself safe here, safe because that juvenile infatuation was long over. Incredibly, it seemed that it had been transmuted into something deeper, more dangerous.

'You couldn't get near the truth about me,' she said tautly, holding herself stiff within the circle of his arms. Loose they might be, but she knew better than to try to escape from them.

Slowly he drew her closer until she was pressed against him, her body sensitised by his caresses so that she could hardly bear to draw breath because her breasts moved against the hard wall of his chest. Wherever they touched small fires were ignited, waiting only for her to lower the barriers in her mind to spring into violent flames.

Conal was not unaffected. So close she could feel his heart, and it was picking up speed, thudding heavily. He bent his head and touched his mouth to the delicate junction of neck and shoulder. Catlin stared at the soft stuff of his shirt, furious with him for subjecting her to this torment, dismayed because he had been right. Here, with the masculine scent of him filling her nostrils, with the hard length of his body in such intimate juxtaposition to hers, his mouth moving sensuously over her skin, she found to her horror that she was not repelled by him. In fact, she was visited by an erotic vision of how they had made love, the ecstasy conjured by his hands and mouth on her body, the hard driving strength of his virility enveloping her, so that until he had entered her and the pain had overwhelmed her she had felt a passion as strong as his.

Now, held against him like this, that passion was waiting only for her mind to slip the bonds of shame before it sprang once more into full, vibrant life.

'Please let me go,' she said harshly, holding herself as erect as she could without arousing his hunting instinct by pulling away.

'Kiss me first.'

'*No*, Conal.'

His breath was warm against her skin, drying the path his tongue had left.

'Yes, Conal,' he mimicked, a lazy note of insolence threading through his voice. 'What's the matter, darling? Afraid you might learn to like it?'

'You can't torment me into—into doing what you want.'

'No, but I could seduce you into it.'

His words forced her backwards and as she had known would happen, his arms tightened forcefully, crushing her against his body. He was aroused, wanting her, hatefully her body responded to his open ardour. Warmth began to spread through her from that tight knot deep in her loins.

'You wouldn't——' she muttered frantically, pushing at him with her hands. 'Conal, you wouldn't!'

'There's a vast difference between rape and seduction,' he said, subduing with insulting ease her attempts to free herself. 'Perhaps it's time you learnt that difference.'

'*No!*'

'Then kiss me.' As her struggles ceased he smiled, his mouth hard but not as hard as his glance. 'That's all, Cat.'

'Why?'

His lips tightened. 'Because I want you to.'

She closed her eyes, shutting out the sight of his cold triumph. But doing that meant that immediately she became more conscious of the smell and texture of him, the hard strength of muscle and bone beneath the warm silk of his skin, the slow movement of fingers as they traced down her spine.

Taking a deep breath, she found his mouth with her own, intending to keep it firmly closed. Useless, for his lips teased hers apart and helplessly she surrendered that stronghold. Conal's arms did not tighten, but his heart began to race as he plundered the sweet depths.

Heat scorched her skin; she swayed, keeping herself upright by clinging to his shoulders.

He made a sound deep in his throat, shifting his position so that he could hold her head more comfortably, one hand tangled in the amber silk at the base of her neck, the other pulling her hips against him. She twisted away, rejecting such overt masculinity, and he thrust against her, punishing her withdrawal with the brutal intensity of his need.

Catlin trembled with shock and fear and an answering ardour. He kissed her throat, his mouth moving with languorous sensuality over her skin. She was visited with the devastating impression that he was tasting her, using all his senses to absorb the very essence of her body. She opened her eyes, but he was too close for her to be able to focus. One hand held her clamped to him so that she could feel every muscle and sinew, taut, waiting, it seemed to her bemused brain, for her to surrender.

'I kissed you,' she pleaded huskily, giving him that surrender. 'Please let me go now.'

His head stilled, then he lifted it and looked down at her, his mouth twisted in a cynical smile.

'It didn't hurt much, did it?' he said, releasing her.

She swayed, but he made no attempt to support her, merely stood watching her from narrowed eyes.

After a moment she said numbly, 'I'm going to bed.'

'And I,' he returned with cool deliberation, 'am going for a swim. With any luck it should take the place of the traditional cold shower and team games.'

Incredibly she flushed, not with anger but embarrassment, and tried to hide it by turning towards the door.

'You know, for someone as sophisticated as you, you blush remarkably often,' he remarked insolently.

She snapped, 'I think with you I regress. Goodnight!'

'Goodnight, darling.'

'Don't——'

'I'll call you what I want, my heart.' It was a threat, softly spoken.

Catlin made her way up the stairs to the sound of his taunting laughter.

Once in bed, of course, she didn't sleep until Conal came up several hours later. By then she was so tired that she dropped off to the soft sounds of his movements through the wall and slept heavily until Jenny came to wake her the next morning.

After that the days moved quietly past until the end of the week. Emily made good progress. The doctors began to speak of only another week or so until she would be able to leave hospital for a convalescent home. Conal saw her every day and was able to reassure Jenny of her grandmother's welfare.

'May I see her on the weekend?' Jenny asked.

He nodded. 'Of course. She's looking forward to a visit from you.'

But not from Catlin. When Saturday arrived Jenny and Conal went into the hospital to see Emily while Catlin walked through the Winter Gardens. Surrounded by enormous cypresses and cascades of bougainvillea, the two huge glasshouses were approached by a flight of brick steps. Once on the wide platform excavated from the side of the hill it was like another kingdom, an enchanted place where goldfish swam in a mosaic-tiled pond between the glasshouses, and an enormous pergola about it sheltered Victorian statues of nymphs and goddesses, smug and gracefully posed on their pedestals.

In the hothouses the growth was tropical, with great palm trees reaching high to the roof and loops of creepers and clusters of vivid, exotic flowers in a lush, fecund atmosphere. With the sun adding its heat it was too hot to stay there for long, so Catlin walked through the gully which had been planted in that other great Victorian craze, ferns, then waited beside the pond watching the thin elegant jets of water from the fountains and the sinuous, red-gold glitter of the goldfish. It was warm and still. She took off her jacket and stood smiling as a tot of about two made her way towards her. An adorable little blonde, she flirted with enormous green eyes, bestowing the kind of smile which was guaranteed to coax an answer from the most ardent child-hater.

She came running unsteadily along the terrace, then a swift backwards glance made her sway. Catlin bent and took her hand and was rewarded with another beaming smile and a chuckle.

'Lalage!'

Her father appeared in the door of the hothouse, gazing around anxiously before he noticed her clinging to Catlin's leg. He came towards them, young and good-looking, half-smiling.

'I say, I'm sorry! She's like quicksilver. Thanks very much for grabbing her.'

'She's a real charmer, isn't she?'

He grinned, a picture of pride. 'We think so,' he said and held out his hand. 'Come on, Daddy's girl, let's find Mummy.'

'Mummy.' The little face broke into a smile. Still clasped to Catlin's leg, she said firmly, 'Tiss.'

'Oh no, not now, sweetie. Come and kiss Mummy.' He looked a trifle embarrassed. 'I'm afraid she's going through a very affectionate stage. She calls every woman Mummy and she likes to kiss them.'

'But she's enchanting. Of course she can give me a kiss!'

Catlin stooped and picked her up. Two surprisingly strong arms clamped themselves around her neck and a moist effusive kiss was pressed to her cheek. Then Lalage held out her arms to her father and said charmingly,

'Fin' Mummy now.'

As they went back to the hothouse the child waved her little starfish hands in farewell. Catlin felt a pang of bitter envy. Some people, she thought, as she watched their reunion with an obviously pregnant Mummy, had all the luck. A happy marriage, an enchanting child, the kind of love which had irradiated that young man's face when he looked at his daughter—all would be denied her for ever. When Conal had taken her so angrily he had diverted her awakening needs. She had found it impossible to trust a man enough to feel safe in his presence. The one or two men to whom she had been attracted since her flight had, on closer appraisal, failed to measure up to some impossible standard she had formed.

What she had been searching for, she realised now, was a man who was superior to Conal in every way. Stronger, with greater magnetism, more handsome, more ruthless, probably even richer. But of course there was no one like that. The peculiar combination of characteristics which made Conal was Conal's alone, not to be repeated.

So it seemed that she was doomed either to waste the depths of her desires in a series of evanescent affairs or go alone through life, an affectionate aunt to other people's children, finding what companionship she could with friends and her fulfilment in her work. Well, plenty of people had done just that and made a very satisfactory life. So would she.

'Catlin!' Jenny's voice, clear and high, ripped through the heavy air. 'Catlin, you look lonely there. Whose little girl was that?'

Slowly Catlin turned, banishing her recent thoughts with a determination which made her sound briskly at odds with the day.

'Her name was Lalage, and in sixteen years' time she's going to break hearts.'

Jenny had run ahead of her father. As he came up she asked a little wistfully, 'Will I break hearts too?'

Catlin's heart smote her. With a quick hug she said cheerfully, 'Hundreds of them, if that's what you want.'

And indeed, the child showed the promise of great beauty, with her father's eyes and fine bone structure and the chestnut hair which was a heritage from her mother, so cruelly dead when she had barely reached her twenty-second birthday. Once Catlin had asked Conal about Claire and he had turned on her, demanding with savage pain that she never speak of her again.

He would be past that dreadful numbing grief now, but his heart was buried in Claire's grave. It was the kindest interpretation to be put on his affairs, so casual and cruelly frequent.

'Did she give you a kiss?' Jenny demanded.

'Yes, she did.'

'Why?'

Catlin laughed, turning a little so that Conal's shrewd gaze took in only her profile. 'Because she wanted to.'

Jenny said fiercely, 'Bend over,' and when Catlin did she kissed her on the same cheek.

'You're not her mother,' she said gruffly, 'you're mine.'

Jealousy, Catlin thought with dismay, carefully avoiding Conal's gaze. 'Darling, I don't really feel like your mother,' she began. 'Why not think of me as a kind of aunt? Or a biggish sister?'

Jenny had retreated to stand behind a statue. Her voice was muffled as she retorted, 'Because I don't want an aunt or a sister. Not a big one, anyway.' She reappeared, obviously struck by a splendid idea. 'I'd love a little one,' she said eagerly. 'Or a baby brother.'

This time Catlin's glance flew to meet Conal's. She read a sneering amusement there and something she couldn't discern unless it was a kind of tenderness for his small daughter before he said, 'You'll have to leave that sort of thing to us, Jenny. Now, if Catlin's ready to go I'll take you up to the Museum coffee shop and treat you to one slice of Black Forest gateau each and then we'll go out to Henderson. I want to buy some wine.'

'Oh, good!' Jenny skipped up to take his hand. 'Will we be going to the Radichs'?'

'Yes.'

'Goody, goody, goody! I haven't seen Karen for ages and ages.'

'Three weeks,' Conal explained to Catlin teasingly, taking her arm as they came down the steps.

It was ironic that Lalage and her parents should be going slowly ahead of them, doubly ironic that behind the smiles that they exchanged Catlin should have noticed a trace of envy in the other woman's face. Not bitter envy, just a little pang at the obvious wealth, the superb physical presence of Conal and Catlin, the blazing physical magnetism and air of authority which he wore so effortlessly.

If you only knew, Catlin thought wearily.

The Black Forest gateau was superb, the Radich family were charming, warm and gay and frankly surprised at Conal's introduction of her as 'my wife.'

'Which you must excuse,' Marija Radich said when Catlin was helping her with the afternoon tea. 'We had heard about you, of course, but you don't seem at all like . . .' She broke off, obviously confused.

Catlin forced a smile. 'Six years is a long time,' she said, spreading whipped cream over a sponge of such height and lightness that she felt that she should be chaining it down.

'Well, you are back now, and that is all that matters,' Marija said comfortably.

Catlin opened her mouth to disabuse her of this idea, but Jenny and Karen came in wailing because the guinea-pig had escaped, and there was no chance then or later when they rejoined the men.

All in all it was a pleasant afternoon. To walk the sponge off they went down the rows of vines while Stefan explained winemaking to Catlin, and then it was time to go.

As they drove off with the Radichs' farewells in their ears Jenny said smugly, 'I do like going there. Karen and Simon are going to the theatre next weekend, Daddy. They asked me if I wanted to go, but I said no.'

'Why?'

She wriggled, hunching her head down between her shoulders. 'Oh, I can go to the theatre any old time,' she said vaguely. 'Catlin, where do you live in 'Stralia? Is it very far away?'

It was easy enough to see the trend of her thoughts. Taken by one of childhood's violent fancies, she wanted to spend as much time with Catlin as possible. Catlin's heart ached for the child, but she refused to allow herself to vocalise her sympathy. When she had gone Jenny would forget, or perhaps a better way would be to keep in touch by letter and card. Most children adored getting mail.

Conal had been remarkably amiable all afternoon. No double-edged remarks, no taunting glances to make her uneasy. Catlin sighed, thinking she should be wary. He was, of course, up to something and she rather had an idea what that something was, but she wasn't going to allow herself to be lured into making another ghastly mistake. One in a lifetime was enough. If he thought that it would be easier to take up with his old wife rather than search out a new he could just think again!

Not even to herself did she admit how perilously easy it would be to allow his expertise in lovemaking to seduce her into his bed and subsequently into his life.

'You're looking very fierce,' he said unexpectedly as they swung off the motorway.

'Thinking. I'll have to write to Deb.'

'Deb?'

'Deb Munroe, the girl I flat with. She'll be wondering what's happened to me. I expected to be back home by now.'

Conal laughed softly. 'Did you? You'd better ring her tonight. Or won't she be home on a Saturday evening?'

'Probably, at least until seven or so. But it will cost the earth.'

'Not so much. Surely you don't want her to worry.'

So she rang. Deb was astounded and then extremely suspicious. 'You did say, didn't you, that you loathed the man?'

'I did.'

'Well then, what are you doing in his house?'

What indeed? 'I'll tell you later,' Catlin said warily before she explained about Emily's illness and Jenny.

'You're becoming *involved!*' Deb hissed. 'I hope you know what you're doing.'

'So do I.' Footsteps outside the room made her look up. 'I'll have to go, Deb. I'll write.'

'You'd better! And listen—you be careful! It sounds to me as though you've put your head into a trap.'

'Or my foot into the lion's mouth,' Catlin agreed, laughing, so that when Conal came into the room she appeared relaxed, even gay.

He lifted an eyebrow at her. 'All's well, I gather.'

'All's very well,' she said sweetly. 'Deb's holding the fort.'

'And how is the boy-friend?'

For a moment she did not know what he meant by the jeering question. Then recollection of the mythical lover she had flung in his face came to her and she said calmly, 'Pining, but he'll manage.'

'Trusting soul. What's his name?'

'That's no business of yours.' She got to her feet and came out from behind his desk; she had taken the call in his study. As she passed him he caught her by the wrist and leaned back against the desk, preventing her from leaving the room.

'Is he so infatuated that you have no worries about how long you leave him?'

She bit her lip but answered coldly, 'Three weeks is hardly an age! Unlike some men, I can trust his fidelity for that long.'

'Three weeks?'

She looked sharply upwards, met his unsparing

scrutiny without flinching. 'That's all the time I've got. My holidays only last three weeks, Conal. If I don't go back then I'll probably get shown the door.'

'What does your lover do?'

'That's no business of yours, either.'

He smiled grimly. 'Most people would consider that my wife's lover is very much my business.'

'It's not most people's business either,' she retorted, intensely scornful. By now her mythical lover was beginning to assume concrete proportions in her mind. She could see him, tall and dark with a rock-steady dependability, kind and masterful and witty. A sudden smile lit up her eyes.

Conal muttered something beneath his breath, something that wasn't quite soft enough. The imprecation made her gasp as he jerked her off balance, clamped her against him and kissed her with a relentless, controlled menace, crushing her lips against her teeth until in self-defence she was forced to open her mouth to his invasion.

A long time later she wrenched herself away, one hand pressed to her ravaged lips, her eyes great gold pools of hatred.

'Don't you touch me ever again!' she said harshly.

'I'll touch you when and where and how I want to. You *brat*, smiling, thinking of your lover!' He stared at her then looked down to where his hand flexed, the knuckles whitening against the skin as he controlled his instinctive urge to hit her.

'At least I don't flaunt him at you,' she spat. 'Remember Belinda? Everywhere we went she was there, draping herself over you, making it so obvious that you and she were very, very good friends. Did you think I was so stupid I couldn't see? Even if I had been there were enough of your friends who were only too eager to tell me—hint, hint, hint, until it was a miracle I didn't scream with hurt and frustration!' She stepped up to him, so angry now that she was no longer afraid. 'And

I'll bet there's someone else tucked away—not too far away—now. Because you can't stay celibate, can you, Conal? You need a woman, any woman so long as she's beautiful and unmarried and wanton, because you don't ever want to get into an important relationship again. Well, good luck to you, if that's what you want, but don't you try to make me feel guilty. What I am you made me. If you don't like it you've only yourself to blame!'

He was white beneath his tan, the hard angular lines of his face intensified into a look of eagle-like ferocity. When he spoke his voice was silky. If she hadn't recognised the terrible anger she might have thought that he was amused.

'Just what do you mean when you say I don't want to get into any sort of meaningful relationship again? No'— as she turned away—'tell me. I want to know.'

Suddenly exhausted, she responded heavily, 'Simply that since Claire died you haven't wanted to fall in love again.'

Conal closed his eyes, then opened them again to focus on the pale, strong lines of her face. 'I loved Claire,' he acknowledged grittily. 'I'll always love her. But she's dead, and although I grieved for her long and deeply I'm not neurotic enough to bury my heart with her. Is that what you've thought all these years?'

'It seemed the most charitable interpretation of your behaviour,' she said stiffly, aware that in spite of the anger and pain of this confrontation they were communicating for perhaps the first time in the farce that was their marriage.

'Charitable? Well, yes.' He took a deep breath and colour began to seep back into his skin as that devastating anger faded. 'But why should you seek to be charitable, Catlin? I'd have thought that the last thing you viewed me with was loving kindness.'

Hesitating, unsure of how to cope with him in this

mood, she turned her head away, veiling her eyes with her lashes.

'Look at me,' he commanded softly, and when she refused took her chin and turned her head towards him.

Still she kept her lashes lowered, although colour burned along her cheekbones, suffused her throbbing mouth.

'Just how did you feel about me?' he asked. 'Why did you marry me, Cat?'

'Because I didn't know what else to do,' she said baldly.

'And because you were in the throes of your first teenage infatuation.'

Well, of course he must have known. No doubt he and Belinda had laughed over it.

'That too,' she admitted, refusing to reveal the sudden unexpectedly raw pain that assailed her.

He said sombrely, 'You had a hard time of it, I'm afraid.'

'So?'

He shrugged, releasing her. 'I should never have brought you here. Never have married you, but certainly not have expected you to fit into my life without preparing you in some way.'

She smiled with considerable irony. 'I've always assumed it was a temporary aberration on your part.'

'Oh, not temporary,' he returned, eyeing her with the bland mockery she so hated. 'No, Cat, far from temporary, I'm afraid.'

CHAPTER FIVE

AND JUST what Conal meant by that only he knew, and he certainly wasn't saying. Jenny's voice calling from the kitchen sent them both there. She had begged for hamburgers for dinner and had happily prepared the meat patties, but she wanted company while they grilled.

Dinner was a pleasant meal. Once more Conal set out to be amiable, and Jenny was delighted to be eating in the kitchen.

'And hamburgers!' she exclaimed. 'Gran doesn't like me eating hamburgers.'

'Once in a while won't hurt.' Catlin handed her a bowl of tomatoes. 'Always provided you have salad with them, of course.'

Yes, dinner was pleasant. Afterwards Conal had to go out. 'Show the flag,' he explained. 'I won't be long.'

Whatever he had to show that flag at was a formal occasion, for he wore a dinner jacket.

Catlin received a quick lesson from Jenny in working the very impressive stereo in the music room off the drawing room and sat down on the sofa, sighing with pleasure to listen to a Palestrina Mass, delighting in the rich sonority of the music and the unmannered fervour of the singers.

The telephone intruded, but she grimaced with resignation and answered it.

A woman's deep, purring voice. 'Is that Mrs Loring?'

'Mrs Conal Loring, yes.'

A moment of complete silence before the unknown said in a voice rather lacking either richness or purr, 'There must be some mistake. I mean——'

'There's no mistake.' Catlin allowed herself to sound a little bored. 'May I take a message?'

'Why—why, yes. Could you tell your—Conal, that Moya Southcott would like him to contact her immediately.'

I'll bet, Catlin thought waspishly as she wrote on the pad by the telephone before saying, 'Right, I've got that. Goodbye.'

'Just a minute. You *are* Conal's wife?'

No purr by now. Just a shell-shocked woman.

'Yes.'

'But—I thought you—I mean, aren't you divorced?'

'No,' Catlin replied firmly. 'Goodbye, Miss Southcott.'

Not even Palestrina's music could calm her now. Prowling restlessly as a cat, she made her way around the small room, picking up and putting down ornaments, savagely angry. Useless to try and reason herself out of it. Certainly Conal owed her no loyalty. There was nothing but a legal tie holding them together, yet the thought of him in another woman's arms had the power to drive her to a blind, gritted-teeth fury.

Facing facts squarely she confessed that it hurt, too. If she closed her eyes she could still summon up that memory of him and Belinda Scargill in the big bed at the beach house, still feel the shock and anguish, the gut-wrenching, tearing agony which had driven her to put twelve hundred miles between them.

Would she never forget? Oh, she had been infatuated with him then, her poor little adolescent heart placed carefully where he could most conveniently stamp it underfoot, but not now, surely? Not now, six years afterwards. The infatuation was gone. Why not the pain?

Just what was it that he had done to her in the few short months of their marriage which prevented her from cutting free of him now? In torment she closed her eyes. The basic attraction was still there, the desire to mate reduced to its most animal, fundamental level. Conal felt it too. If she was willing she could be another affair, one that he would enjoy as much as his others and with exactly the same result, boredom and then a callous farewell.

Slowly she forced her lashes up and stared at the small-paned French windows. They were old and the glass was irregular so that her reflection was distorted. Through it she could see the moon rising behind the feathery leaves of a tamarisk.

Was that what he wanted? To revenge himself on her for that flight six years ago? With precision, as though cogs were clicking into place in her brain, she realised that only that would explain his behaviour since she had arrived here. Was he cruel enough to use that reluctant attraction as a reprisal for the humiliation she had made him suffer then? She bit her lip, admitting reluctantly that he was capable of it.

Catlin made a thick, urgent sound in her throat, pressing cold hands to colder cheeks. Behind her Belafonte's voice flowed smoothly, hauntingly, across the room. Like every other room but hers in this house this one was beautifully decorated, warm and comfortable and expensive, with furniture and ornaments which had grown together in friendship over the years. Her reflection in the window looked alien to it, tall, restless with a kind of bristling, brittle energy that sent her thick mane of hair flying behind her. Pacing out her torment, she tried to organise her thoughts into some sort of order.

He wanted her here. Why? She had thought he was being bloody-minded, but Conal never did anything without a good reason. As well as her need for his approval of her plans, he had used Jenny's growing affection to persuade her to stay; how like Conal, she thought on a sneer, to make use of the daughter he loved. Even his mother's illness had played into his hands.

Too astute not to recognise her unwilling, repressed attraction, he had used that, too.

That first night when he had kissed her, her revulsion had shaken him, hurt his pride, and he had deliberately made love to her, forcing her to realise that he was correct, it was not him that she was afraid of but her own tumultuous response to his sexuality. At least, she thought, shivering with emotion, she had not admitted it to him, although he must know.

Was he wooing her, trying to infiltrate her defences? That first night he had said that he needed a wife, perhaps he thought that she was now mature enough to be a suitable Mrs Conal Loring. Did he want a besotted wife, so caught up in his toils that she would be complacent enough to ignore the inevitable affairs on the side? Well, I've got news for you, she muttered, pushing her hand across her tired brow. Perhaps he thought that his greatest revenge would be a docile wife, too busy producing children and caring for them to worry about his extra-marital love life.

Wife or affair, whatever he wanted, he'd have to learn to do without. She had no intention of fulfilling either function. This lion, she thought with grim humour, was definitely going to be the one that got away!

As the record stopped she hurried across to turn the stereo off; it would be stupid to stay up as if she were waiting for him.

So she was in bed with the light out when he came back. A quick glance at the luminous dial of her watch revealed that he had been away for just two hours. No doubt he had glanced at the telephone pad so he would know that Moya Southcott had rung. Not that it would worry him. After all, he was quite used to coping with a mistress and a wife simultaneously.

Catlin sighed, stretching. Of course the sultry-voiced Miss Southcott—or Mrs—could well be a mere business acquaintance. It was just highly unlikely. Smiling cynically, she drifted off to sleep.

And woke to a miserable day, heavy, sullen clouds threatening with a cold snivelling wind from the south-east.

'Brr!' Jenny shivered, turning to her father. 'Can we put the heating on? I'm frozen!'

'It's already on.' He ruffled the dark hair. 'Give it time.'

'Where are we going today?'

He looked across at Catlin. 'I'm going to work in the study, I'm afraid.'

'Oh, *Daddy*!' Poor Jenny didn't attempt to hide her disappointment. 'Do you have to?'

''Fraid so, darling.'

Catlin said calmly, 'I'll tell you what—Easter's coming up soon. Why don't we make Easter eggs?'

Identical eyes regarded her with identical questioning looks.

'Can we?' Jenny asked doubtfully.

'Let's see what we've got in the kitchen.'

As they left the room she felt Conal's eyes on her back. Something in the cold gaze made her uneasy, but once in the warmth of the kitchen she forgot it in the fun of initiating Jenny into the delights of making her own Easter eggs.

An hour or so later Conal came in, admired their efforts so far and waited until his daughter's excited chatter died down before saying, 'By the way, Catlin, we're going out tonight.'

'Oh?' Her head lifted, the skin at the back of her neck prickling.

'Yes.' There was definitely mockery in the deep voice now, but he looked perfectly calm and reasonable. 'Remember the Gregorys, Elaine and Phil?'

Catlin's lips tightened as she nodded. Only too well she remembered them!

'I saw Phil last night. I'd promised to go to a party at their place tonight, a reception for a trade delegation from Peru. Elaine's just rung to ask if you'd like to come, so I accepted for you.'

'Kind of you.' Catlin's voice was stiff with resentment. Phil Gregory was a big bluff hearty man with a basically kind nature corrupted by the exigencies of a business career; his wife was sleek and gracious and malicious. No doubt she was consumed with curiosity at the sudden reappearance of Conal's child bride.

He knew, of course. He laughed and touched her cheek, ignored her definite withdrawal. 'They usually give good parties. You'll enjoy it.'

So Mrs Jansen's Karen arrived with her load of books, grinned cheerfully at Catlin and kissed Jenny. While Jenny watched, fascinated, as Catlin got ready the babysitter unpacked her overnight bag and prepared for a marathon sitting with her prep.

'Catlin,' said Jenny wistfully, 'I wish I had ginger hair like yours.'

Catlin grinned. 'Darling, yours is perfectly beautiful.'

'My mother had black hair too.' A little sigh, then the high clear little voice continued, 'She was very beautiful, my mother was.'

'I know. More important, she was a darling.'

'Did you know her?'

'No.' Catlin pulled her dress on over the smooth green slip which had won Jenny's hearty appreciation. 'No, but I heard a lot about her.'

'Who told you?'

Catlin smoothed the deep green silk into place.

'Your gran, mostly,' she said absently. Once she had anguished over Claire's manifest perfections as detailed by Emily. Now Claire's poor little ghost no longer worried her.

'Did she?' Jenny sighed. 'She doesn't tell me much about her, and Daddy doesn't either.'

'You've never asked me.' Conal had come through the connecting door, tall and elegant in evening dress, his expression impassive.

Jenny wriggled. 'Gran said not to.'

He frowned. 'Darling, you may ask me anything you want about your mother. I promise you I won't mind,' and as Jenny's mouth opened on an obvious question he grinned and went on, 'But not now, sweet. It's time we went and Catlin is, as always, late.'

'I'm ready,' she said in mock-indignation, pretending for Jenny's benefit. 'See?' She pirouetted so that the graceful folds of silk swirled around her legs.

'No!' Jenny cried. 'You haven't put perfume on.'

So Catlin sprayed herself with 'Fidji' and then sprayed Jenny.

'Right, now I'm ready,' she said calmly.

'Not quite.' Conal unfolded his hand and held it out to her.

Something glittered and winked in the hard palm. Catlin felt the colour drain away from her skin; she stood without breathing as he skilfully hooked in the beautiful things.

'Earrings!' Jenny crowed happily. 'Oh, Catlin, they're beautiful! All yellow and white and sparkly. You look like a princess.'

'Out of the mouths of babes,' Conal said softly, holding Catlin's gaze with his own until the colour rushed back into her cheeks and she looked away, unable to control the wild tumult of sensations which his closeness and the touch of his fingers on her ears sent churning through her.

'And you look like Sleeping Beauty,' he said, turning to his daughter, but not before Catlin had seen the glint of satisfaction in his eyes. 'Off to bed, Jenny.'

They spoke little in the car. Catlin was too bemused by the knowledge that he had kept the earrings he had given her for her eighteenth birthday to be conscious of the silence; her thoughts kept her busy.

It wasn't until they were almost at Remuera that she remembered Moya Southcott's call—and mentioned it, curiosity driving her into what was probably an indiscretion.

'Yes, I saw the note,' Conal said blandly. 'Thank you for taking it.'

A question hovered on the tip of her tongue, was ruthlessly suppressed. She would not show any further curiosity.

The Gregorys lived in an enormous modern house set on the right side of Remuera Road with a magnificent view to the north over the suburbs and the harbour. When Catlin had come here before it had been brand new and too conscious of it, but since then trees and gardens had grown and the house had achieved a mellow air of being at one with its surroundings.

'Catherine!' Elaine Gregory's voice expressed astonishment; she could not hide it, and Catlin's heart swelled.

'Actually,' she returned, giving her her hand, 'my name has always been Catlin. How are you, Elaine? You look well.'

'My dear, you look ravishing!' Malicious laughter glittered in Elaine's dark eyes. 'Conal, doesn't she look ravishing? Phil, here's Catherine, whose real name is Catlin. Don't you think Australia agrees with her?'

While Phil was shaking her hand and agreeing with everything his wife said Catlin smiled, and realised that such an effusive welcome could mean only one thing. Conal's latest mistress, whoever she was, was definitely in evidence tonight.

The Peruvian delegation were charming. Catlin enjoyed their excellent English and the dark Latin skill at unspoken compliments, but her antennae were alert. And an hour or so after her arrival she met the vivid green eyes of a stunning blonde.

One look from the exquisitely beautiful creature—the kind of look she had never forgotten—and Catlin knew who Conal's woman was.

Oh dear, she thought, unable to prevent exasperation and anger as the blonde's eyes swept over her. Oh dear. And a few other choice complaints.

Of course Elaine appeared, choosing with a perfect

sense of timing which Catlin would have liked used in a better occasion, the exact moment when Conal was talking earnestly with the head of the Peruvian group.

'My dear, here's someone who's been dying to meet you,' she said, detaching Catlin with superb skill. 'Catlin, this is Moya Southcott. Moya, Conal's wife, Catlin.'

And stood back to watch events with her own particular brand of malicious amusement except that Phil called her away and she had to leave the two women alone.

'*You* are Conal's wife?'

The sharpness of the question attested to the other woman's astonishment.

'Well, at the moment,' Catlin replied crisply.

'Oh.' A short silence before the older woman said, 'You must excuse my surprise. I'd heard—at least, you don't look anything like I'd imagined you to be.'

'Frustrating, isn't it?' Catlin decided to extract the utmost out of the situation. 'Don't you find it often happens? I'm always being terribly disappointed by reality.'

'Well, yes—I mean, no. It's just that from what Conal said I'd thought you to be completely different.' Her tone invested the words with heavy significance.

Irony gleamed golden in Catlin's gaze. 'Ah, but he hasn't seen me for six years,' she said blandly. 'I suppose he remembered a schoolgirl. A lot can happen in six years.'

'Oh, it certainly can.'

More significance. Moya's incredibly long thick lashes drooped suggestively over her eyes, making a spiky shadow on the smooth perfection of her cheeks.

She really was beautiful. Not, perhaps, profoundly intelligent, but then almost certainly Conal hadn't chosen her for her brains.

Catlin was beginning to enjoy herself. Clearly Moya thought that she had prior claims and she was trying to get the idea across without actually saying so. Well, good luck to her, but if it actually came to a contest Catlin would put her money on Angela Perrott. Every bit as beautiful and probably just as stupid, she had Emily's backing, and that was a powerful advantage.

'What do you do, Miss Southcott?'

The other woman gave her a swift sharp glance. Colour touched the matt skin. Catlin felt rather guilty; she hadn't meant to be condescending, but that was the way her query had sounded.

'I'm in fashion,' she said. 'And you?'

Catlin told her.

'Oh,' Moya Southcott said thoughtfully, 'how clever you must be. Do you find much prejudice against women in your work?'

'None. Plenty of women in Australia take up accountancy. There must be a lot here, too.'

Moya nodded. 'It sounds incredibly boring, but I suppose if you have that sort of brain. . . ' She laughed, looking sideways as Conal stopped beside her. 'I'm afraid I'm far too frivolous for that sort of thing, aren't I, Conal darling?'

Catlin tensed. In spite of herself she could not forget the pain that used to assail her when Belinda Scargill had spoken to him in just such an intimate tone of voice, coupled with that swift, sideways glance which had shut his wife out, making her feel gauche and foolish and insignificant.

That was six years ago, she reminded herself, and said brightly, 'Oh, surely not *frivolous*, Miss Southcott? I don't think you should put yourself down like that; no one should ever think of themselves as paltry, or trumpery.' She smiled at the baffled anger in Moya's expression, adding helpfully, 'That's what it means, you know; silly, without sense. If you go around calling yourself names like that someone might believe you. People do tend to take you at your own valuation, unfortunately.'

Moya looked stunned, as well she might, Catlin thought unrepentantly. Seldom had she ever been so flagrantly rude, and seldom had she enjoyed anything more. In a way she was revenging herself on Belinda and those friends of Conal's who had stripped her of her self-confidence all those years ago. It was a pity that poor Moya had left herself open for it, but if she hadn't tried that slyly conspiratorial glance at Conal she wouldn't have been slapped down so severely.

It was he who spoke into the tense little silence, saying with cool assurance, 'I'm sure Moya hadn't intended such a literal use of the word; she was giving it its commonly accepted meaning. Can I get you something to drink, Moya?'

'Oh, darling, thank you, I'd love one. My usual, please.'

He looked at Catlin, eyes cold and mercilessly promising punishment. 'Catlin?'

She smiled, shaking her head so that the light caught in her smooth yellow-amber hair. For a moment there was an aureole about her, gleaming in the lamplight, each strand glittering like fire.

'No, thank you,' she said, her glance insolent, slyly catlike.

'Your hair is quite incredible,' Moya said as he moved off. 'What do you use to keep it that colour?'

'Soap.' Catlin allowed a note of boredom to creep into her voice. 'Conal teases me about looking like a lioness.'

At this moment a voice squealed out joyously across the room. '*Cat!* Cat Galbraith, of all people! What are you doing here away from your mountains?'

Laughing, her expression suddenly vivid, Catlin turned to receive a tiny body as it hurtled into her arms.

'Easy, easy!' she said, hugging with almost as much enthusiasm as she was being hugged. 'Maxie Horrocks, for heaven's sake! What on earth are you doing here?'

'I was dying of boredom until I saw you towering

over everyone else. Oh, Cat, you look absolutely *super*! Where have you been all these years?'

By this time Conal had arrived back, delivered her drink to a bewildered Moya and was watching with amused comprehension.

'Conal *darling*!' Maxie enthused now, holding her face up for a kiss which she returned with immense enthusiasm. 'Conal, do you know Catlin——?'

He laughed, his eyes meeting Catlin's in a shared moment of unholy mirth.

'Yes, darling, I do know her. As it happens, she's my wife.'

Maxie's vivid green eyes widened to their greatest extent. *'Wife?'* she demanded in the clear ringing tones which had everyone in the room listening openly. 'But, darling, how did——? Oh, you mean *Cat* is the child bride who left you!'

Conal put his head back and laughed, as did Catlin. It was impossible to be offended by Maxie's frankness. She was laughing now with them, her small face alive and vital above her tiny slender body.

'But how incredible,' she gurgled. 'I used to go and spend my holidays with Cat when we were kids, but we lost touch! At least I lost touch. I didn't answer your letters, Cat darling. I'm *so* sorry. But my dear, I'm married now too and *pregnant*!' She beamed at them and patted her slender waist. 'Three months and not a single minute of morning sickness. I feel quite cheated. Where's Red?'

Red was her husband, tall and quiet and elegant, clearly devoted to her. When the introductions were being made Moya was at last able to join in the conversation, which she did with a slight air of deference which puzzled Catlin until later, when they were able to gossip quietly, Maxie enlightened her. 'Red is rolling with money,' she said, laughing delightedly, 'and he owns the agency where Moya works.'

'Oh.'

Maxie looked shrewdly at her but said nothing.

After a moment Catlin grinned, 'We can't talk here. How about coming to lunch tomorrow?'

'Yes, please. I am,' Maxie said plaintively, 'dying of curiosity, but I think I might be able to contain it until then. Oh, Cat, it is lovely to see you again! And you look so super! I always used to envy you that little air of—of competence that you have.'

Catlin laughed but refused to tell her the joke, and as Conal and Red Layton, whose real name was Russ, were coming towards them that was the end of the matter.

Much later, when the Laytons had gone, Catlin wandered out of the hot, too-close room on to the wide terrace and stood for long moments looking up at the sky. Clear across it spread the gauzy band of the Milky Way. In the east the Scorpion, winter's constellation, was rising, sting poised as it chased Orion the summer hunter below the western horizon. Glowing redly in the scorpion's body was Antares, which the Maoris call Rerehu. In the Southern Hemisphere when it is overhead before midnight it is winter.

By the time that happened Catlin would be back in the warmer climate of Australia. She sighed, leaning back against the smooth grey trunk of a silk tree, its light-sensitive leaves folded against the night. It was late, after midnight, but the city still hummed with life. Once she had hated Auckland, wept bitter tears for her mountains and rivers. Now . . . well, perhaps maturity dulled that keen sense of belonging. Or perhaps she had learned to extract the most pleasure from that which must be endured. As she listened to the faint noise of the traffic and the more vigorous noise coming from the rooms behind her she sighed once more. Australia seemed very far away, as far away in distance and time as her childhood home.

After a moment she straightened up, shivering. Stupid to allow herself to be overcome with nostalgia for a time when she had been bitterly unhappy!

Before she could move from beneath the darkness of the tree two people came out on to the terrace. She stiffened as she recognised them and turned her head away, but there was a shrill note in Moya's tones which carried across the quiet air.

'When,' she asked, 'am I going to see you again?'

'I don't know.' Conal's voice was noncommittal, without emotion.

'How long is she going to stay, for heaven's sake?'

'That's none of your business,' he said.

After a long pause Moya said in a trembling voice, 'I suppose now she's here you don't want to be bothered with me any more.'

'That's hardly the thing to be discussing here, is it?'

Catlin shivered, recognising only too well the flat forbidding note in his deep voice. You're trespassing, it said quite clearly. Move off.

Like the young Catlin, Moya recognised it too. 'Very well,' she said, striving for dignity. 'I'll ring you tomorrow.'

'I'll be busy all day, I'm afraid.'

Don't let him do it to you, Catlin felt like screaming. He's a swine and he'll break your heart, you stupid little fool. Against the rich material of her dress her hand clenched, crushing, the knuckles white. By the time she had regained full control of herself they had gone back inside.

Not much later, when she had returned inside and was parrying the not too serious advances of some man, Conal came over and said curtly, 'Time we went, Catlin.'

'Oh, no, I should have known,' her would-be swain moaned. He was slightly drunk. 'Go away, Conal, you can't have a lien on all of the most attractive women. Where's Moya? Didn't I——?'

'Gone,' Conal snapped, suddenly emerging from behind the sophisticated mask to reveal a man who was savagely angry. 'And this is one woman I have a definite lien on. Catlin happens to be my wife.'

There was a moment's silence before the other man said in horrified tones, 'Heavens! I say—I'm sorry. I didn't realise . . .'

'Of course you didn't,' Catlin soothed to ease the situation. She smiled at him, mischief lurking in her eyes. 'I'm the migrating sort of spouse, very rarely here.'

'Shall we go?' Conal had her elbow in a grip which permitted no appeal.

'Surely.' She smiled again before allowing herself to be urged towards the door by fingers which were suddenly cruel.

During their thanks and farewells she could feel his anger beating at her, although the mask was firmly back in place.

Once in the car he said coldly, 'I'd appreciate it if you didn't flirt quite so obviously with anyone who takes your fancy. You know, we gave them enough to talk about tonight without your amatory activities as an extra bonus.'

She chuckled. 'You sound just like a husband! A rather pompous one; vaguely Victorian, in fact. And,' with a sudden bite of acid in her voice, 'like most Victorians, a hypocrite.'

'Moya is not——'

'My concern? Of course she's not, and I wouldn't have mentioned her if you hadn't decided that your pride was in danger. Because that's all it is, Conal. It hurts to think that your wife, whom you have no interest in at all, could show any interest in another male. Unworthy of you.'

'Is it?' The words were drawled out as, with customary efficiency, he overtook another car on the way to the toll booth.

When he handed over his card she looked across at the hard beautiful lines of his profile. For a sensualist his expression showed an immense amount of self-command, the full lower lip held firmly in check by the thin upper and the determined, angular jaw.

'You know it is,' she said quietly when the car was again in motion. 'All possessive male—but really, it's the dog in the manger, isn't it, Conal? Sorry, but I refuse to play. I'm not your possession.'

Even in the dimness of the car she could see the flash of his smile, appreciate the irony of it.

'You know, for someone with the amount of experience you claim, you know very little about the male ego,' he observed musingly. 'Possibly because you grew up without watching how your mother coped with your father. You bear my name, Cat. That makes your behaviour of considerable interest to me—and to everyone else at that damned party tonight. Didn't you notice how they watched us?'

'Of course I did.' Scorn gave an edge to her voice. 'I don't care about gossips. Neither do you, or you wouldn't make your affairs so obvious.'

'Moya is not an affair.'

In spite of herself Catlin's brows climbed. 'No?' she said sweetly. 'Are you sure she realises that?'

'Like you, I haven't lived a life of unsullied purity since you left——'

'Or even before I left,' she interpolated neatly.

'—but Moya is not my mistress.'

'Well, well! She certainly does her best to give that impression. She's in love with you. Presumably you've taken her out fairly frequently—and given her some reason to feel jealous and hurt at my unannounced arrival.'

'Catlin,' he said, very softly.

'Yes?'

'Are you trying to goad me into losing my temper?'

An involuntary shiver turned her skin cold. 'No. I remember rather vividly what happened the last time I did that.'

'If you don't want to risk a repetition just leave the subject alone, will you?'

'What an easy way out for you,' she retorted.

'Threaten me with rape to shut me up. End of discussion.'

'Were we discussing?' He was crisply sarcastic. 'I thought you were hurling abuse at me. If you must know, I have slept with Moya, several times. I gave no promises, I took nothing she didn't offer eagerly. I made it quite clear that I had no intention of embarking on a serious relationship. Right from the start she knew of our marriage. She's in love with my bank balance, not me, and she's had as much of that—and me—as she's going to get. Satisfied?'

For some strange reason Catlin felt sick, but forced her voice into some semblance of normality. 'Oh, more than satisfied. Only she doesn't seem to quite understand the situation, does she? Is that why you wanted me over here, Conal? To get rid of her?'

There was a long, taut silence before he muttered in a furious undertone, 'My word, that's some powerful death wish you've got there! If you have any instinct of self-preservation at all you'd better keep quiet until we get home.'

Which Catlin did, telling herself that she had pushed her luck enough for one evening.

In retrospect it hadn't been too bad. At least she had forced a few reappraisals of her character. As well as the Gregorys several of Conal's friends who had once been intensely patronising had been there, and it had given her an immense amount of enjoyment to watch them readjusting their attitudes. Meeting Maxie again was a pure bonus!

A smile softened her mouth. Maxie Horrocks had been her only friend, sent out to the station almost every holiday for three years by parents who were too busy with a social life to bother about her. Together they had ridden and skied, swum and made mischief, forging bonds which still held. Maxie's warmth and shattering candour had been fascinating to the quiet, reserved child who had been Catlin. She had been desolated when after a divorce Maxie's mother took her to England with her and there were no answers to her letters.

Lost in her memories of some of their more exciting exploits, she hadn't realised that the car had come to a halt.

'You're smiling,' Conal said softly.

Suddenly relaxed, she told him why.

'I can imagine,' he said with dry emphasis. 'She's led Red Layton one hell of a dance.'

'He doesn't seem to mind.'

'You don't need to sound so defensive. He's besotted with her, as I'm sure you saw.'

Catlin smiled ruefully. 'Everyone always was. She could get away with anything short of murder, and frequently did. I could never understand why her parents were so aloof and unloving.'

'They had a particularly messy divorce. I imagine that neither of them had much emotional capital to spare at that time. Did I hear you make a lunch date with her?'

She looked across sharply. 'Yes. Why?'

'No reason,' he said softly. 'Do you plan to spend the rest of the night here?'

'What? Oh, no, of course not.'

But she fumbled with the catch of her safety belt, muttering beneath her breath when it stuck.

'Here, let me,' Conal offered. 'I'll have to get it replaced—it sticks too often.'

Catlin snatched her fingers away as his hand moved over hers. It took him a moment or so to free it, his dark head bent, absorbed in the small task. He moved with such deftness and fluidity that nothing he did was awkward or unbalanced; that splendid relaxed masculine grace had been one of the things which so intimidated her when they lived together.

When it was done he looked up suddenly, catching her watching him. At the back of the vivid blue of his gaze something glittered.

'You look tired,' he said evenly. 'Faint shadows under slumbrous eyes, that peculiarly boneless air one acquires when one is exhausted. There's only one more thing missing . . .'

Mesmerised, she stared unmoving as his head blotted out the small light in the car. His lips were warm and seeking, pressing against her bottom lip until she opened her mouth for him. Even then he did not force her into the kind of kiss she feared. With heart-stopping gentleness he explored her mouth, finding the sweet depths as if that was all that he had ever wanted.

Catlin's heart beat thickly in her ears. Without volition, a prisoner of the exquisitely sensuous feelings he aroused in her, she raised her hand to touch his cheek, her fingertips thrilling at the slightly rough warmth. He lifted his head and slid his arm further around her shoulders, then tipped her chin so that the pale gleam of her throat was bared to him.

His mouth was sweet torment against her skin, finding the most sensitive areas with a sure skill gained through many such encounters in the past. Tiredness made Catlin's brain move sluggishly; before she had had time to realise her danger he had seduced her into a dazed surrender.

His hand slid beneath her arm, holding her gently yet with purpose. As his mouth moved back to hers, teasing her with little soft kisses, his other hand stroked the length of her throat, finding the pulse that beat its betraying tattoo beneath her ear and then in the vulnerable hollow at the base of her throat.

Something strange was happening to Catlin. She felt weightless, a warmth spreading from her loins to her limbs, rendering her helpless. Her breath caught in her throat, she moved, jerking her head back, afraid of the reaction this would cause.

But he whispered, 'Quietly, darling, quietly,' and she relapsed back into quiescence, trembling yet strangely secure.

Slowly, as his mouth traced the contours of her face, his hand moved along the fine bones of her shoulder beneath her dress. She could feel the leisurely, loving sweep of his fingers as they shaped the smooth curves. Against her his heart beat heavily, with an increasing rate which at last penetrated the sensual mists of her brain.

'No,' she said thickly through lips which seemed swollen and slack.

To her astonishment his hand stopped its roaming, pushed aside the neck of her dress to expose the swell of her breast above her slip. His mouth swooped and then he said with a note of rather forced casualness in his voice, 'That's how you should look, Catlin. Ready for love.'

Harshly, assailed by shame at her swift surrender to his practised seduction, she demanded, 'Don't you mean sex?'

'The two can be synonymous.'

'Not in this case.'

He let her go as she moved to get out of the car, but she had to wait at the door while he locked up, and when he came up to her he said calmly, 'You see, Catlin, you're not so different from Belinda and Moya and all those other women you despise for falling for my "meretricious charms".'

The bite in his words drove the colour from her cheeks.

'Did I say that?'

He smiled without humour. 'Yes. The never-to-be forgotten night before you left me. That's why you were so angry, wasn't it? Because you desired me in spite of the fact that you hated me.' As the key turned in the lock he added blightingly, 'In fact, that's why you hated me.'

He had it wrong, of course, but she could not tell him that. Not even yet was she ready to confess that she had been stupidly, recklessly obsessed with him, at the mercy of a passion so strong that the only way she could control it was to hide it, bury it deep beneath the weight of years. And then it had taken only a week or so in his company for that painful attraction to force itself upon her again, as strong as ever.

Harlequin reaches
into the hearts and minds
of women across America
to bring you

Harlequin American Romance.™

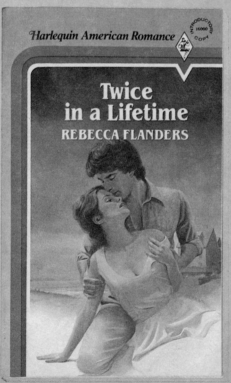

Enter a uniquely American world of romance with
Harlequin American Romance.™

Harlequin American Romances are the first romances to explore today's new love relationships. These compelling romance novels reach into the hearts and minds of women across America...probing into the most intimate moments of romance, love and desire.

You'll follow romantic heroines and irresistible men as they boldy face confusing choices. Career first, love later? Love without marriage? Long-distance relationships? All the experiences that make love real are captured in the tender, loving pages of *Harlequin American Romance*.

What makes American women so different when it comes to love? Find out with *Harlequin American Romance!* Send for your introductory FREE book now.

GET THIS BOOK FREE!

MAIL TO:
Harlequin Reader Service
2504 W. Southern Avenue,
Tempe, AZ 85282

YES! I want to discover *Harlequin American Romance*.
Send me FREE and without obligation, "Twice in a Lifetime."
If you do not hear from me after I have examined my FREE
book, please send me the 4 new *Harlequin American Romance*
novels each month as soon as they come off the presses. I
understand that I will be billed only $2.25 per book (total
$9.00). There are no shipping or handling charges. There
is no minimum number of books that I have to purchase.
In fact, I may cancel this arrangement at any time. "Twice
in a Lifetime" is mine to keep as a FREE gift, even if I do
not buy any additional books.

154-CIA-NAD4

Name   (please print)

Address   Apt. No.

City   State/Prov.   Zip/Postal Code

Signature (If under 18, parent or guardian must sign.)

Experience *Harlequin American Romance*...

with this special introductory FREE book offer.

◀ SEE EXCITING DETAILS INSIDE

Send no money. Mail this card and receive this new, full-length *Harlequin American Romance* novel absolutely FREE.

CHAPTER SIX

THE HOUSE was warm and quiet, a dim lamp in the hall lighting them to the stairs. Karen, the babysitter, had long since gone to bed.

'You're wrong,' said Catlin, one hand on the banister.

He looked an enquiry at her, stopping her progress by trapping her hand beneath his warm one on the polished wood.

'I don't want to discuss it now.' She hesitated, looking down at their hands before ending. 'I don't think there's anything *to* discuss. Six years is a long time, Conal.'

'Not long enough for you to grow up.'

Anger sparked in her eyes. 'Did I challenge you tonight? What was it I said that made you decide to see if I could be had?'

'You are a challenge in yourself,' he answered smoothly, his expression shuttered as he watched the rapid rise and fall of her breasts. The penetrating blue gaze moved back to her face, pinning her there open to his scrutiny. 'But I don't need to tell you that, do I? You know it already. It shows, that consciousness of yourself as a desirable woman, that aura of sleek promise. How many lovers did it take to give you back your confidence, Cat?'

'How many for you?' she parried. 'You have it too. I always thought it was inborn, but perhaps it comes from satisfying hundreds of women.'

His fingers tightened on hers, cruelly implacable, until he swore under his breath and lifted his hand away. 'Don't ask for trouble,' he said thinly.

'Then don't attack me. I no longer have to take whatever you care to dish out.'

'Six years hasn't taught you discretion where I'm concerned either,' he said harshly, jerking her down the two steps into his arms. They closed tightly around her, forcing her into such close proximity that she could feel the dark force of his virility against her. Its counterpart within her body, the traitor deep inside her, reawakened into sudden life. It took all her self-control to hold herself stiffly, to ignore the sudden aching heat in her loins, the urgent desire to press herself against him and let passion take over.

Feverishly she tried to summon from the past the fear and humiliation of that night before her flight, but her memory betrayed her so that all she could recall was the piercing sweetness of his hands and mouth as he had explored her body, the unsatisfied yearning which had soon suffused her being.

Turning her head so that she was no longer half suffocated against his chest, she said fiercely, 'Let me go, Conal!'

He made no attempt to kiss her, but when she spoke he bent his head and touched his lips to her forehead before releasing her. 'You,' he said deliberately, watching her as she turned to go back up the stairs, 'are going to end up driving me mad.'

It seemed best to ignore the ragged note in his voice, and as she checked Jenny before preparing for bed Catlin forced her brain to dwell on the party, on her reunion with Maxie—on anything but the moments she had spent caught in his web of desire.

But later, as she stared into the darkness with blind, hot eyes, she remembered Belinda Scargill, who had had short, geometrically cut red hair and the body of a tigress, slender and sinuous and voluptuous. Her enormous blue eyes had always lingered on Catlin in a kind of incredulous contempt and she had spoken to her with a patronising sweetness which still made Catlin squirm. How she had hated her! Belinda was everything that Catlin longed to be and fell so flamboyantly short of.

She had known, of course. The entire progress of the affair had been played out before her deliberately blank gaze. Night after night she had lain in this very bed, cold with despair because everyone knew that Belinda and Conal were lovers and thought she was unaware of it. Very vividly she could remember the conversations which had stopped so abruptly, the snide allusions, the sly sideways glances and half-concealed smirks.

And now, for whatever reason, he desired his errant wife. Serves him right, she thought viciously, toying with the idea of deliberately leading him on and then paying him back for that old humiliation by turning him down flat.

Only for a moment, however. The role of tease was not for her. And retribution would be swift. And cruel. Conal wasn't the sort of man to be teased with impunity. She sighed and turned on to her side, wooing sleep with closed eyes and conscious deep breathing. It was years since she had lain like this, dwelling on past wrongs. Soon after her flight she had decided that brooding was totally unproductive, self-pity despicable, and had refused to allow herself to indulge in it.

Still, it was sensible to remember just how bitterly he had hurt her before. Harbouring grudges was uncivilised and bad for the character, but those moments spent in his arms in the car had been perilously sweet; it was time to reorganise her defences.

Pain tore through her. Oh *hell*! she whispered into the pillow, weeping softly so that he wouldn't hear. Why had he insisted on her coming back? Playing God, forcing her from the safe happy life she had made for herself just for mischief, or to appease a guilty conscience.

When he had seen her again he had wanted her because she looked elegant and sophisticated, worthy prey for such a notorious hunter. And she, stupid idiot that she was, had told him that she was experienced, so he wouldn't feel any remorse at stalking her, reactivating the basic chemistry that had always been there. Surely he could tell that beneath that polished veneer she was still as innocent as that young girl who had fled him?

Oh, she had been so stupidly *confident*! So arrogantly sure of her own strength that she hadn't really worried about the danger into which she was walking!

The worst part of it was that she should have known. Otherwise, why would she have spent these last six years living like a nun? She had thought that the pain of her initiation into sex had frightened her, but of course it hadn't been that at all. Simply that Conal had so stamped his image on her subconscious that she was unable to love again. There had been a couple of men for whom she had felt a spark of attraction, but although she could probably have enjoyed their lovemaking she was unable to enter into a casual affair and neither of them had measured up to her rather stringent standards.

Standards based entirely on Conal, she realised now. It was stupid to pass over a man because he had the wrong sort of voice or gesticulated a little too much when he spoke. Both of them had reminded her slightly of Conal, although the resemblance ended in a similarity in colouring and build and that awareness of feminin interest which so angered her in him.

Devious swine, with his warm tender kisses, the teasing infiltration of his hands! She was not going to give him the chance to seduce her. Let him, for once, suffer the pangs of unrequited desire. It would do him no harm to find out what it was like!

Maxie arrived in a vivid scarlet car which clashed luxuriously with her mop of red curls.

'*Darling!*' she called almost before she climbed out from behind the wheel. 'Hey, Cat! I'm here!'

'Coming!' Catlin was laughing as she suffered the shock of Maxie's embrace once more. Anyone else would have been considered too demonstrative; Maxie got away with it because she possessed something of the candid openness of childhood.

'Well, here I am,' she said cheerfully, 'and I warn you, I'm absolutely *agog*! Did you know our men are attending a meeting together today?'

'No, I didn't. Conal and I don't talk about business.'

'I'll bet!' Maxie laughed at her hostess's face. 'Oh, darling, don't be stuffy. You know you can't keep it up. Even when we were kids I could always coax you out of your fits of nobility. I was impossible then and I haven't changed.'

Catlin laughed, remembering just how impossible she had been, and how loyal and trustworthy. Maxie never told tales or used her blatant charm to get favours for herself alone, although she wasn't above playing on it to help them avoid the natural consequences of their pranks.

'Come and sit down,' Catlin said, leading the way through the house to the terrace.

'Mm, very nice. Red and I live in an enormous modern affair clinging to a precipice in Titirangi with kauri trees coming in through the window and six-inch wetas making their solemn way across the breakfast table.'

'Ugh!' Catlin hated the enormous brown crickets found in the New Zealand bush.

'Well, I don't mind them as much as the huhu beetles at night. The other night one flew straight down the front of my nightdress!'

'Oh, yuk! What did you do?'

Maxie giggled. 'Screamed. Red ripped off my nightie with considerably less ceremony than he usually does and killed the beast. And the next day a truck climbed up, and I mean climbed, because our drive is *vertical*, and fitted screens to all the bedroom windows.'

Their laughter blended on the clear slightly salty air. Mrs Jansen brought out white wine, refused some herself with the cheerful confession that it gave her appalling headaches, and bustled back in to see to the lunch.

'Live-in?'

'No,' said Catlin.

'She seems a sweetie. I've got a dragon who watches me like a hawk in case I do something to imperil the future heir to the Layton fortunes. She's a darling, too, but a bit like a nanny.' Maxie took a large mouthful of wine, let it slide luxuriously down her throat and said, 'Ah! Now tell all. First of all, how did this Catherine Loring I heard whispers about suddenly turn out to be the dearest friend of my childhood, Catlin Galbraith?'

So Catlin gave her a necessarily expurgated version of the truth. Maxie listened, sipping quietly at the wine, her expression oddly tranquil for someone whose features were so charmingly mobile.

'Well, that's the edition for general purposes,' she said when Catlin had finished. 'What really happened?'

'Can't you guess?'

'Yes, I'm rather afraid I can. What on earth was he thinking of, marrying you? He must have known that it wouldn't work.'

Catlin shrugged. 'I think he was still in shock after Claire's death. He was very deeply in love with her. Still is, if it comes to that.'

'Doesn't sound like the Conal I've come to know and love. Who was the woman?' At Catlin's blank look Maxie smiled. 'Oh, come on, darling, I know him well. And you. Obviously something drove you away, and it must have been something pretty fierce, because you are simply not the type to turn your back on anything you call a responsibility.'

'A woman called Belinda Scargill.'

Maxie frowned. 'Never heard of her. What was she like?'

Catlin described her.

'Poor Cat! No wonder you cut and ran. Still, you're back now, and that's all that matters.'

'Not permanently.'

This met with considerable surprise. 'Who says? That was very definitely one possessive man last night, as our Moya saw and hated.'

'She's one reason,' said Catlin with a faint snap in her tones.

Maxie's enormous eyes opened to their widest extent. 'But Cat, that's over now—has been for ages!—and let's face it, you can't blame the man. She chased him quite unmercifully from the moment she laid eyes on him. He wouldn't be normal if he hadn't taken what she was so blatantly offering.'

'What would you do if Red was unfaithful to you?'

'That,' Maxie said stubbornly, 'is a different story. I'd kill him—I think. But you weren't here, you left Conal six years ago. I mean, you can't really blame him for an occasional affair.'

'Occasional?' The one word was a masterpiece of scorn.

'Yes.' Maxie was watching her carefully, her vivid little face sober. 'Truly, Cat, he's not a lecher of the first degree. I mean, I've been here four years and known him for three of those and I can think of only one other woman his name has been linked with. And you know what Auckland's like. If there had been anyone else I'd *know*! In fact, exaggeration is the norm, as you well know.'

'There's Angela Perrott,' said Catlin with stubborn disbelief.

Dismissing her with an airy wave, Maxie said persuasively, 'Everyone knows that Emily Loring has been trying to bring that off, and everyone, even Emily, knows that it's hopeless. It's been hopeless with all the other nice, well-bred girls she's paraded in front of Conal. He doesn't want to marry again.'

'He can't,' Catlin snapped. 'He's not divorced.'

'Why not?'

Catlin shrugged. 'I don't know. Presumably because married he's safe from Moya Southcott and her kind.'

Maxie whistled. 'Boy, you've certainly got it in for him, haven't you?' There was a long silence broken only by the soft hoot of a launch siren out in the channel. Then Maxie said softly, 'You must love him very much.'

'I don't—I hate——' Catlin broke off in confusion, staring at the woman opposite with horror. Then as realisation hit her she dropped her head, covering her face with her hands, and stayed like that for long silent minutes.

Of course Maxie was right. Catlin had been fighting a rearguard action ever since she had been hijacked to this house, shadow-boxing against her own inclinations and desires, refusing to admit to the deep, turbulent love which had been kindled in her over six years ago by a man who had no idea of what he had done to her.

'I thought it was infatuation,' she confessed at last, sitting up straight and looking at Maxie's warm, compassionate little face. 'Stupid, isn't it? I must be like those baby geese that acknowledge the first thing they see as their mother. I'm fixated on my first love.'

'Couldn't he be your last love, Cat? I'll swear he wants you.'

'As he wanted those others? Would you be happy to live a marriage like that?'

Maxie sighed. 'No, I suppose not. Yet you go so well together, a perfect match. Red was saying that he hoped you'd make Conal happy. He's very fond of him.'

'Oh, Conal's immensely lovable.' Catlin scowled at her glass, at the pale straw-coloured wine, and suddenly tossed it off.

'To hell with it,' she said, blinking back sudden tears. 'Let's have lunch. I set the table in the dining room, but let's bring it out here. It's too lovely a day to waste indoors.'

They spent the rest of their time together reminiscing, laughing like the two schoolgirls they had been, Maxie's outrageous sense of humour fuelling their conversation, until just before Jenny was due to arrive home she sighed and made her farewells.

'No, I've got to go, or my darling dragon starts ringing around,' she said cheerfully. 'Oh, Cat, it's good to see you again! I wish you'd stay. I've made stacks of friends here, but old friends are the best, aren't they.'

'No chance,' said Catlin. 'But I promise not to lose touch with you again.'

'Some men,' Maxie said ominously, 'don't know when they're lucky. I love Conal devotedly. He makes even my matronly heart go pit-a-pat when he smiles at me, but I could give him a good *kick*! Never mind, Cat, don't give up. Hang on in there!'

Catlin smiled wryly. 'No,' she said calmly. 'He knows that I've no intention of staying here.'

'Well, you know your own business best, I suppose.' But it was clear that Maxie was dubious of this. However, she possessed the priceless asset of knowing when to stop, so she said no more but gave Catlin a final hug and took herself off in a small spurt of gravel after arranging to meet again.

Sighing, suddenly oppressed by a nameless fear, Catlin made her way back into the house.

Mrs Jansen was frowning as she put the telephone receiver down. 'That was Mrs Loring,' she said absently. 'She wants someone to take her some things— books to read, and a fresh nightgown.'

Catlin frowned. 'Conal will have to take them over tonight.'

'Have you forgotten? He's having dinner out and going to visit her before he comes home.'

'Oh.' Catlin's frown deepened. 'Well, I suppose I could,' she decided. 'As it's not visiting time I won't be seeing her, but I could just hand them in at the ward and ask someone to get them to her.'

Mrs Jansen's face cleared. 'Well, if you could,' she agreed. 'She wants notepaper and things too. I think she must be bored. She's not used to lying about and she'll fret if she's kept too still for too long. When is she going into the convalescent home?'

'Next Tuesday, if all goes well.'

Catlin glanced at her watch. 'Look, you know where her things are kept. Could you make up a parcel and I'll take them over now. I want to get back before Jenny gets home. She's going to ballet with Joanne Henderson and her mother; Mrs Henderson rang and offered yesterday, but I'd like to be here when she gets back.'

Twenty minutes later Catlin was taking the small Mercedes which was Emily's car along the motorway, her forehead pleated as she kept in mind the differences in the roadcode she was used to and the New Zealand one. After Sydney traffic Auckland's held no horrors for her, but she was determined not to let a moment's lapse of concentration put the car in jeopardy.

She got there safely, parked in the car park and made her way to the building where Emily lay. It should have been a five-minute effort, but the Sister came past as Catlin was giving the parcel to a nurse.

She stopped and said pleasantly, 'Why don't you give it to her yourself, Mrs——'

'Loring.' Catlin was flustered. 'I'm her daughter-in-law.'

'Well, come along. She had no visitors this afternoon and is feeling a little down.'

Catlin looked helplessly at the nurse but couldn't find words to explain her problem. At last, when the silence had stretched almost to embarrassment, she nodded, and followed the kindly and interfering Sister.

Emily was sitting up in bed; her expression did not change when she saw Catlin but her voice was cool as she greeted her and she did not offer her cheek.

'You're looking well,' Catlin observed, taking a chair.

'I'm feeling extremely well.' Emily moved position. 'How is Jenny?'

'Oh, fine. She misses you, of course.'

'Naturally.' Another silence. Then, 'Conal looks tired.'

'Does he? I hadn't noticed. He doesn't seem to be spending too much time at the office.'

'He finds your being here a strain. Why did you come back?' Emily looked at her with determined dislike.

Catlin blinked, realising with surprise that her mother-in-law had screwed up her courage to ask her this.

'Was it money? If it was, I've a little . . .'

'It was, but I can assure you that I didn't want to come back. Conal forced me to.'

Emily lay back, her expression contemptuous. 'I suppose he felt that as he was putting up the money he was entitled to see how you'd got on.'

'Possibly, if he had been putting the money up. It is mine, you know. Conal is merely the trustee. And,' Catlin added with a snap, 'he won't be that for much longer. I'm going to get him replaced by someone a little less intimately connected to me.'

A noise from the bed made her lift her head in astonishment. Emily was laughing. 'Do you really believe that?' she asked, and this time there was scornful pity in her glance as it rested on Catlin's suddenly pale face. 'My dear girl, your father's estate was swallowed up by death duties and debts. You've been living off Conal all these years.'

Catlin's breath hurt her lungs. For a moment the room swung hideously about her. She felt the colour drain from her face and dimly, in the distance, heard her mother-in-law exclaim something.

Slowly the blackness before her eyes faded. Emily was staring at her, one hand pressed to her mouth.

'Good heavens, you didn't know!' The whispered words were harsh. 'Catherine, for heaven's sake—where are you going?'

'Away.'

As she walked down the corridor she heard Mrs Loring call out again, but she ignored her, concentrating only on setting one foot before the other in a straight line. A nurse looked curiously at her and stopped, watching her until she turned a corner.

Catlin walked from the hospital down through the Domain, careless of the beauty, the restful peacefulness of her surroundings. Slowly, moving like a woman delivered a mortal blow, she made her way through the streets, blanking her mind until she could get to her lawyer.

When the car stopped beside her she took no notice, her eyes bent on the ground. Even when Conal ordered her to get in she stepped on, shivering.

'Get in,' he said again, but this time he was beside her, big and determined.

She looked up at him with dull, lacklustre eyes. 'I want to see Mr Stretton.'

'I'll take you there.'

He touched her gently, urging her into the double-parked car, locking the door before he swung around the front and slid into the driver's seat. Catlin sat with her head bent, her fingers folded loosely together in her lap like a schoolgirl. She felt numb, her head stuffed with clouds, unable to think beyond the fact that her splendid new life had been built on the patronising largesse of the husband she loved and despised.

When the car stopped she looked up, bewildered.

'We're here,' he told her, unclipping her seatbelt as if she were a child.

She shrank back and felt his swift anger, but all that he said was, 'Do you want me to come in with you?'

'You might as well.' Her voice was impossibly remote, a high, little-girl's voice. 'I have no secrets from you, apparently.'

His hand dropped to cover hers. 'Catlin . . .' he

began, but she moved swiftly out of the car on to the footpath.

Clearly Mr Stretton had been warned. He looked guilty and upset at the same time, his elderly face set in lines of worry.

'My dear,' he said, waving her to a chair. 'My secretary has made you some coffee. Won't you drink it?'

'Yes, of course.'

He exchanged a look with Conal and went on quietly, 'Now, Mr Loring tells me that unfortunately you heard the—you were told about the real state of your affairs without any warning.'

Not until then did Catlin realise how desperately she had wanted it to be a lie. The coffee trembled in the cup as she stared down into it.

'Yes,' she said after a false start. 'Will you please tell me exactly how much I—where I stand?'

Later, when the shock had receded a little, she would discover that it wasn't so bad. At its inception there had been very little in the trust, but Conal's skilful husbanding of her resources had increased her capital considerably.

'You will end up by being quite a wealthy young lady,' Mr Stretton said soothingly.

As though that mattered!

'So—so the income that I've been getting . . .?'

Again that swift glance exchanged with Conal, invisible behind her. 'Yes,' the lawyer admitted reluctantly. 'When I first got in touch with Mr Loring he revealed the true state of affairs to me and we agreed on this scheme.'

'I see.' And she did, too, far more than poor Mr Stretton did. 'And did you also agree to keep him up to date with my activities?' she asked coldly.

Mr Stretton shook his head firmly. 'I did not, beyond reassuring him that you were well and happy.'

'Thank you for that, at least.' She rose to her feet and

held out her hand, saying with quiet dignity, 'Thank you for all that you did, Mr Stretton. It can't have been a particularly pleasant position for you to be in.'

He made soothing noises at her, and bowed them out. As she sat back in the car seat Catlin remembered numbly, 'I left the other car in the hospital car park.'

'Don't worry about it. It's being dealt with.'

'Of course.' Well, of course it would be; Conal was an expert at dealing with things. Runaway poverty-stricken wives, importunate girl-friends, trusts, lawyers —nothing confounded him.

Suddenly she covered her face with her hands and stayed like that until they reached home, her eyes dry and tearless.

Once there Conal picked her up and carried her up to her bed, ignoring her protests with a face of carved stone.

'Get into your night clothes,' he commanded. 'I'll bring you something to drink.'

'Mr Stretton gave me coffee.'

'Do as you're told.'

She shivered, her fingers plucking at the satin cover. 'Very well,' she replied dully.

When he returned she was lying in the bed with her arm over her eyes as though the light hurt them. He had poured brandy into hot milk, repulsive to taste, but as she obediently sipped it down it warmed the cold inner reaches of her body and her shivering stopped.

'Try to get to sleep,' he said, so she turned her head into the pillow and, incredibly, slept.

It was almost dark when she woke. Outside the sun was setting and there was the murmur of the waves on the beach. She lay quietly, somewhat muzzily reflecting on the fact that the waves seemed louder at dawn and sunset. Somewhere on the road a child rode along ringing a bicycle bell, the shrill noise softened by distance. Jenny laughed out on the lawn, then called the dog. Her clear high voice blended with the little excited yips that were Patch's answer; a moment later both sounds broke off and Catlin smiled, knowing that the child's face would be buried in the dog's warm furry neck.

Closer at hand she could hear Conal speaking. On the telephone in his room, clearly, and to his mother.

'I'll ring you as soon as she's awake,' he said, a little impatiently. 'Yes, I know, Mama ... Yes ... yes, I'll tell her ... Goodbye.'

The connecting door was wide open; through it she could see the dark corner of his bed. Such an austere bedroom for a sensualist!

The sleep had cleared her brain of the numbing fog which had rendered her temporarily witless. Now, lying in his house, surrounded by his possessions, she accepted the fact that since she left him her life had been made possible by his money. Common sense told her that it was blood money, given because he felt guilty about his treatment of her, but at base it all came down to the fact that her valued independence was as insubstantial as air. She would have to reorganise her whole life. The first to go would be her dreams for the bookshop; there was no way that she could afford that. And all her savings must be repayment to him. Then the flat—on her salary as a very junior accountant she would not be able to afford the flat. Deb would have to find a new companion to share with. Her fingers clenched on the percale sheet. How amused Conal must have been by her arrogant denial of his rights! It must have given him an immense amount of secret satisfaction to know that her much-vaunted freedom was due entirely to his support. When had he intended to tell her?

Perhaps he had planned to use her debt to him as a lever to force her into his bed? Even as the thought occurred to her she rejected it. That was not Conal's way. He was too confident of his powers of sexual persuasion to use blackmail. No, he was sure that sooner or later she would succumb to the attraction that flared between them, too sure of it to use force to get her.

A door slammed. Wincing, Catlin smoothed the place where her fingers had crushed the sheet. His voice made her start.

'I thought you were going to sleep through the night.'

She lifted her lashes to watch him come across the room. In a voice which matched his for cool lack of expression she replied, 'No, not this time. How much brandy did you give me?'

'Hung over?' He smiled and sat down on the side of the bed. 'Enough to get you off to sleep, anyway. Feeling better?'

'Yes, thank you.' He was too close, his weight holding the sheet tightly across the bed so that her body was in high relief beneath it. Colour touched her cheeks as his glance lingered on the length of her legs, the flattened mounds of her breasts.

'Good,' he said, smiling as he leaned over to pick up two pillows from a chair. 'Sit up,' he ordered, and when she did he dropped them in behind her.

Catlin dragged the sheet up to cover her breasts and sat there staring at him in mute anger.

'You look about sixteen,' he said, pulling a strand of yellow-amber hair.

She asked harshly, 'Would you have ever told me?'

'No.' He stood up, but only to sit down again a little further away.

'*Why*, Conal? You must have known——'

'That you'd accept nothing from me?' He smiled again, but this time it was without amusement. 'Oh yes, I knew that. What the hell else could I do? You were just eighteen, with no family, no friends to help you. If I'd been able to extract your whereabouts from Stretton I'd have brought you back, but he refused to tell me. It never occurred to me that you'd go to Australia.'

'Why? Because I was too much of a hick to be able to

hold my own?' She spoke bitterly, her face set in anger and pain.

'I thought you'd go back to the South Island. I had detectives looking for you for a year.' He said with a sudden spurt of anger, 'I'd have worried myself sick if I'd known where you were. You obviously couldn't cope with the change from Mount Fay to here. Australia should have frightened the life out of you.'

'Ah, but I didn't have you—or your mother—or Belinda Scargill—to harass me there,' she retorted, head flung back against the pillows. 'There I was free to do as I wanted. I love Australia. It's been very kind to me.'

'And you can't wait to get back.'

'No, I can't.'

Conal stood up and walked across to the window, standing with his back to her as he stared down at the lawn below. Across his shoulders his shirt pulled as though he was slightly hunched.

Without volition Catlin closed her eyes, but his image remained imprinted against her eyelids. Tall and lean, long-legged and slim-hipped, the dark smooth head set proudly above broad shoulders, the hand which held the curtain back slim, long-fingered yet incredibly strong. He swam night and morning, length after length of the pool to keep himself fit, but it was more than that aura of health and strength which made him so attractive.

His voice came to her from a distance. 'Are you all right?

'Yes,' she said, and opened her eyes again. 'I'll get up now.'

'Nonsense!' The shrewd blue gaze roamed her face before he turned away again. Against the light his profile was chiselled perfection, a peculiarly masculine combination of strength and beauty. 'You'll stay where you are until tomorrow morning. Jenny is quite excited. She's going to eat her dinner with you, and tonight you'll be the one who has a bedtime story.'

A tender little smile curled her mouth. 'Very well, then,' she said, resigned to her bed, 'but I'm perfectly all right.'

'You like her, don't you?'

'Jenny?' She looked down at her hands. Above her breasts the green sheet made a folded band across the pale blue cotton of her nightgown. Her arms gleamed golden against the soft cool colours. 'Yes,' she said slowly, instinct warning her not to become too enthusiastic. 'Yes, she's a darling.'

With seeming inconsequence he said, 'My mother is extremely sorry for her behaviour today.'

'She rang you, I suppose.'

'Yes.' He seemed to hesitate, then came back to sit down once more on the side of the bed. He did not make any attempt to touch her, but his glance rested for a long brooding moment on her hands as he said, 'She was afraid that you would do something—she rang me immediately, but I was out. Fortunately my secretary knew where I was and got in touch with me. Why were you so upset, Catlin?'

'You know why,' she whispered, turning her head so that he couldn't see her expression. 'To discover that all these years I'd been beholden to you for *everything*. It made a mockery of all that I thought and said and did.'

'No, how can you say that?' He took her hands, holding them in a warm, comforting clasp, his thumbs gently stroking the blue veins at her wrist. 'Cat, don't be a fool! You don't need me to tell you that you've matured delightfully into a warm, intelligent woman with a rare strength of character. Probably the best investment I could have made with the money!'

Well, perhaps it eased his conscience to say things like that! Inconsequently she asked, 'Where were you when your mother tried to contact you?'

His fingers tightened. Something in the quality of the silence made her look up sharply. Bitterness twisted his lips as he said harshly, 'I was with Moya.'

Anguish shafted through her, making her draw a swift shallow breath. 'I see,' she said.

'No, you don't. I took her to lunch and then drove her home, where I told her that I wouldn't be seeing her any more.'

'Not on my account, I hope,' she retorted with acid composure, hating him, hating herself for being so weak as to be hurt by his blatant infidelity.

Conal swore, softly and beneath his breath, refusing to release her hands when she tried to pull them free.

'No. It was over before you came back.' Broad shoulders lifted in a shrug, the blue of his gaze darkening as she averted her face. 'She knew the rules, Cat. I'm not the first and I won't be the last.'

'She's in love with you.'

'I told you before, she doesn't know the meaning of the word. Oh, she wants me, but she's wanted others.'

'And Angela? What about her? She seems to want you too.'

He slid his hands up her arms, pulling her free from the pillows. His touch was gentle but inexorable, he smiled, but beneath his eyelids there was a glitter she recognised and dreaded.

'She's my mother's choice,' he said softly. 'I haven't slept with her, if that's what you want to know. And I've made her no promises either. Cat, why do you hate my women so much? In any other woman I'd think it was jealousy.'

Beneath the warm cajoling note in his deep voice there was the cold arrow of a taunt. Flicked on her pride, Catlin jerked back from him; he smiled and allowed her to fall back on her pillows, but followed her, sliding his arm around her to imprison her with his weight.

'I am *not* jealous!' she hissed, furious.

'Well, I am,' he said astonishingly, and smiled without humour at her bewildered face. Speaking between his teeth, he went on, 'Jealous of every man who's had you like this, helpless beneath him on a bed. That time I took you I was furious, but not too angry to find you very sweet, a tender little virgin with a quite astonishing talent for lovemaking. I've never forgotten how you reacted when I showed you just what love is all about. Such magnificent abandon, until I hurt you.'

He spoke drowsily, his mouth brushing the silken side of her throat with tormenting gentleness. Catlin drew in a deep breath while beneath the thin cotton of her nightgown her breasts ached, the rosy peaks hardening in betrayal.

'Love?' she stressed. 'That wasn't love, Conal. You were in a flaming fury and you raped me, because you wanted to cut me down to size for daring to yell at you about your sordid little affair.'

He laughed beneath his breath, not at all put out by the scorn in her voice. 'Mmm, that was how it started. But it wasn't long before both of us forgot what had happened before, was it?'

His hand moved gently across her shoulder, the fingers smoothing the soft skin. Catlin stiffened while a singing torrent of fire ran headlong through her body. Against her skin his lips were gentle but merciless, searching out every sensitive spot, moving closer and closer to her breasts. She knew what he would do, knew exactly what her reactions would be to his avid mouth. He had been right when he described her as abandoned. The memory of her shameless passion was so hateful to her that she had pushed it to the back of her mind, refusing to admit that he had known exactly how to send her spinning from her axis into a vortex of passion.

'Don't,' she groaned, doing violence to the aching need which racked her body. 'Please, Conal—I can't bear it!'

He lifted his head to stare at her, but his fingers trailed lightly over the rounded generous curves of her breasts. Deep in his narrowed eyes there was a gleam of mockery.

'Poor Cat,' he said deeply. 'My poor darling. Why won't you admit that you want me as much as I want you?'

'Because I don't!' She slapped his hand away.

Instantly he caught her hair, jerking her head back to expose the vulnerable sweep of her throat and breasts to his gaze. The ceiling light wavered in her gaze; half sobbing, she twisted away, trying to avoid those cruel hands and lips. A quick tug got rid of the barrier of the sheet and he came down on the bed beside her, crushing her into the mattress with the weight of his body.

'Yes, you do,' he said coolly, and kissed her.

Not roughly, not with passion and frustration driving him to cruelty. Gently, oh, so gently, his mouth touched hers in unsatisfying little kisses which tantalised beyond bearing, setting the blood in her veins leaping in a torment of unsatisfied desire.

She held out as long as she could, closing her eyes so that she couldn't see the knowledgeable amusement in his. But then she couldn't prevent the scent of him from filling her nostrils or the feel of him from arousing fires in a thousand pressure points in her limbs and body.

When he realised that she wasn't going to fight him the cruel grip on her hair relaxed and his hand began to caress the nape of her neck. Catlin shuddered, wanting only to feel his weight on her in the sweet agony of complete union. For six years she had refused to remember how it had been that night, but the memory had only been repressed, not forgotten. Now, sighing, signalling surrender with relaxed muscles and an open mouth, she slid her hands across his back, stroking the hard strength beneath the fine material of his shirt.

'I want you,' he muttered, his mouth hot against the soft swell of her breast. 'My sweet torment, you'll drive me out of my mind if you don't let me love you.'

'You took what you wanted last time.' Was that her

voice, thin and dry and vague, her entire attention
focussed on the sensitive nerves of her skin and
fingertips?

'Mmm, and regretted it—oh, so much.' The thin
straps of her nightgown were pushed down her arms,
exposing her breasts to his greedy mouth and eyes. 'Not
this time,' he promised against the pale skin. 'Not ever
again.'

He was gentle, as if afraid to frighten her, but there
was superlative skill in his caresses. How many other
women had lain like this, watching through glazed eyes
as he explored their bodies with hands which knew
exactly how to arouse and excite? Tremors racked her
in an agony of desire; when his mouth reached its
objective she stiffened, remembering that last time it
had been then that she had stopped fighting. Against
her breasts his face burned; his mouth was hot and
demanding, working its black magic as his free hand
stroked the length of her thigh.

Cat's hands clenched painfully on his shoulders.
Waves of heat emanated wherever those tormenting
fingers touched. She tried to remember why she didn't
want to take him to her, why she had been so afraid of
this silken slavery, but her brain was only conscious of
the sensations that overpowered her.

CHAPTER SEVEN

AND THEN there was the sound of footsteps running along the passage and Jenny's voice, high and unaware.

For a moment they lay locked together until, as the door opened, Conal jerked the sheet up to cover Catlin's nakedness. But that was all he had time to do, so that when his daughter followed her peremptory knock into the room they still lay together on the bed, to all intents and purposes lovingly intertwined.

'Oh!' Jenny was startled, but she came further into the room, her blue gaze bold and interested. 'I'm sorry, Catlin, I thought . . .'

Conal had recovered himself. Pushing a hand through his hair, he rolled from the bed, saying coolly, 'You should wait until you're invited, Jenny, before bursting into a bedroom.'

'I didn't know you were in here.' Jenny's glance returned to Catlin as she slid beneath the sheets, embarrassed and so angry with herself that she could barely think.

'I'm sorry, Catlin,' Jenny said again, and then with such eagerness that it hurt, 'Are you going to stay with us, after all, Catlin? You are Daddy's wife really, aren't you?'

'Yes, at the moment.'

What had impelled her to add that qualifier? Shrinking alike from the swift calculating glance that Conal lanced her way and the sudden shadow on Jenny's features, she swallowed, trying to free her throat from the painful dryness at the back of it.

'But you were kissing him.' Jenny was not to be put off. 'And Daddy was kissing you. You were, weren't you, Daddy? Why won't you stay, Catlin? I'll be good, I promise you. I don't care what Joanne says, you *aren't* an awful stepmother like in the books.'

'Oh, darling,' Catlin said helplessly. 'Jenny, it's not you, I promise it's not. I love you—I like you very much . . .' Her voice trailed away. She looked across at Conal, demanding support, but he was standing in the shadowed corner of the room tucking his shirt into his trousers, refusing to help her.

'What is it, then? Why won't you stay, Catlin? Daddy wants you to. I asked him and he said yes. And I w-want you . . .' The sensitive bottom lip began to tremble. 'You make everything such fun,' Jenny finished, gulping as she glared at Catlin with drenched eyes.

'Come here,' said Catlin, holding out her arms.

But Jenny stood like a little statue, blue eyes fierce with a strangely adult hurt. 'I think—I think Patch wants me,' she said, and ran out of the room.

Catlin bit her lip, then turned her face into the pillows. 'Damn!' she said softly, savagely. 'Damn, damn, *damn*!' Lifting her head, she flashed fiercely, 'Now see where your bloody arrogance has led! Why the hell couldn't you have left well alone, Conal? But no, you had to play God and drag me back here, hurting Jenny and ruining my life! And it's entirely possible that your mother wouldn't have had that stroke if you hadn't produced me like a bloody incubus at a feast!'

'Do you think I hadn't thought of that?' he asked harshly. At her stricken face he exclaimed, '*No*, it's not true. Catlin, I swear it's not so. She's had high blood pressure for years, but she's always been very casual with the drugs she's supposed to take. Her doctor said it was only a matter of time before this happened. At least she'll recover fully, and from now on we can only hope that she'll be more sensible.'

Catlin stared down at her trembling hands. 'And what about Jenny?' she demanded bitterly.

'Like Mama, she'll recover,' he said drily. 'Although I'm hoping that she'll be able to persuade you to stay.'

For a moment the words didn't register. When they did Catlin lifted her head to stare at him in a kind of horrified bewilderment. 'I—*what* did you say?' she stammered.

He smiled, apparently amused by her reaction, although his blue gaze was watchful, almost wary. 'You heard.'

'But—but *why*?'

It was impossible to see what he was thinking. The lean intelligent features were shuttered, the heavy sweep of lashes veiling the brilliance of his eyes. Like an enigmatic bronze statue he watched her, the determined, passionate mouth held strongly in check.

'Why not?' he asked coolly. 'You are my wife. Sexually we have all the ingredients of a very good marriage. You've grown up into a woman able to take her place at my side. Jenny has fallen in love with you.'

'While your mother isn't likely to want to act as your hostess any longer,' she taunted, corrosive acid eating at her heart. 'And you wouldn't have to go through the bother and delay of a divorce before you can marry someone equally suitable. Yes, I see what's in it for you. What I'd like to know is, what's in it for me?'

Something tightened in his expression, throwing the angular framework of his face into relief. 'Money,' he said grimly as he came across to the bed. 'And—this.'

She should have known better than to taunt him. It was that which had made him force her, and what he was doing now came close to that ultimate humiliation. As she tried to clamber across the bed he caught her shoulders, dragging her back against him so that her nightgown rolled down around her hips. Conal laughed and bent his head and bit the lobe of her ear while his hands met around her ribs, forcing the rounded globes of her breasts upwards.

'You look,' he said with cold satisfaction, 'like a pinup from one of those magazines you despise for exploiting the female form. With just a little rear-rangement——' and with incredible strength he pulled her, twisting and writhing, from the bed so that her nightgown landed in a crumpled heap around her ankles, 'you look like a still from an X-rated movie.'

Impervious to pain, for she was tearing at his hands with her nails in a frenzy of rejection, he laughed and cupped one breast while his other hand drifted lower, moving from the angle of her hip to the soft depression of her navel and then lower.

'*No!*' Catlin went wild, thrashing about with feet and hands, jerking her head back to catch the point of his chin. Forgotten were the veneers of civilisation; she fought with every aid in her possession until at last Conal exclaimed something and flung her back on to the bed, where she lay gasping and winded, her darkened eyes lit with flames of passionate hatred.

'Very enticing,' he drawled, holding a handkerchief to his cheek. 'You pose extremely well. And if it weren't for the fact that Jenny will probably be back as soon as her pique is forgotten, I'd accept your invitation. I'll take a rain check on it.'

'You will *not!*' She stared up at him with such venom that she was sure her emotion must distort her features. 'I loathe you, you arrogant swine! Don't you dare come near me again, ever!'

'Oh, shut up!'

The bored, chilling tone of his voice hit her like a bucket of icy water in the face. Her hands clenched into fists.

'All that fine fury signifying nothing,' he gibed disparagingly, watching her from beneath half-closed lids. 'You think you hate me, Cat, but what really terrifies you is the fact that more than anything else you want to make love with me. You're as possessive about me as I am about you—otherwise why would you have got rid of my women so quickly and efficiently? You made it quite clear that there's no future for either Moya or Angela. Because you're so bloody jealous, that's why. Sheer, sexual jealousy!'

He smiled insolently as a tidal wave of colour rushed over her skin. 'You're hot for me,' he said softly. 'Greedy for me, craving for me, Catlin. Oh, don't try to deny it, I can see for myself. Your body betrays you whenever I come near you. I'd like to take you, see if I can sate you, but I'm not going to.' Still smiling, he bent down and kissed her, his hands curving under her hips, his face pressed into the taut plane of her stomach. His tongue lingered; shivering, suddenly cold with sweat, Catlin's hands clenched fiercely as her body arched in involuntary, blatant provocation beneath him.

'No,' he said, and straightened up, took the sheet and flung it over her with callous determination. 'No, you lovely sensualist, we'll sleep together when you decide to stay as my wife. Not unless, and not until then.'

Long after he had left the room Catlin lay motionless, eyes closed, the acrid taste of defeat burning in her throat. He was right, of course. When had he ever been wrong in his dealings with women? Devilish, to reduce her to such quivering hunger that her pride was whipped, beaten down beneath a desire which was as elemental as it was powerful. And then to use it as a weapon against her, forcing her to beg and then refusing her what she craved most in the world.

Again bright colour stained her cheeks. With an inarticulate murmur she turned her head into the cool pillow. How could he? He had spoken of her desire, but beneath the cold taunt in his voice there had been a hot tide of hunger equal to hers, held in restraint only by his will. For long minutes she toyed with the idea of seducing him, slipping naked into his bed in the middle of the night when sleep would have weakened his strength of will. But she doubted that it would work, even if she could bring herself to act like a cheap wanton. And if she succeeded he would make her pay.

Shivering, cold with reaction at the thought of just what sort of payment he might exact, she showered, changing into another nightgown and re-making the bed before climbing back into it.

Outside it was dark, the only sound the quiet hum of traffic on the roads. While she had been in the shower someone had delivered her dinner; it waited on a tray on the bedside table. No doubt it was up to Mrs Jansen's usual standard; five minutes after she had finished it Catlin couldn't remember what she had eaten.

Not too long after that Jenny returned. Clearly she had been warned to say nothing more about the future, but after they had taken turns to read a bedtime story she hugged Catlin fiercely before running out of the room.

Catlin wrote a letter to Deb, wryly amused at how easy it was to fill pages with irrelevant news. Fond though she was of her friend there was no way she could tell her about the situation without Deb worrying herself into a tizz.

A small wind blew in from the sea and set the branches of the paulonia tree swaying against the sky. Catlin got up and pulled the curtains across. She began to read, but the words rearranged themselves in fantastic patterns before her eyes, so she turned the light off and tried to relax. It was very quiet. The whole house seemed to listen. Faintly from some neighbouring home came the sound of a record, only the ominous throb of the bass travelling across the intervening distance. It was an eerie sensation, lying there in her quiet, hateful room with the distant beat of drums her only companion. A fragment of long-forgotten poetry came from whatever recess of her brain it inhabited. *'Dim drums throbbing from the hills half-heard.'* Chesterton, she thought, learnt when she was a child. She muttered the words beneath her breath, flinging herself sideways on to the pillows. Her head felt heavy, not quite aching but very close. Several deep breaths later she closed her eyes, trying to summon up sleep.

Ten minutes after that a slight sound brought her upright in the bed, eyes flying open as she strained to see across the room.

'Conal?'

'Yes.' He opened the connecting door. 'I thought you were asleep.'

Fat hope, she thought dispiritedly. 'No.'

'Can I get you something?'

'What time is it?'

He looked at the thin platinum watch on his wrist. 'Nine o'clock.'

Good heavens, it felt like after midnight!

'No, thank you,' she said wearily.

'Goodnight, then.' He withdrew, and she lay there and listened frantically to the soft formless noises which filtered through. Sometimes he swam before he went to bed, other nights he walked along the beach; usually he took Patch with him on these nocturnal walks. Sure enough, a quickly stifled yelp revealed the dog's presence.

Catlin lay tensely waiting for their return, refusing to think beyond that. When her brain returned to Conal's incredible proposition she forced it on to paths of her own choosing, remembering her time at university, the fun of being young. His rape had cured her of her childish infatuation and she had felt like a prisoner after release, slightly drunk with life and living.

So what was she doing even contemplating a return to her prison?

Groaning deep in her throat, she pushed her face into the pillow. She would *not* mull things over any further.

But when the connecting door opened once more she was still awake. Instinctively she lay quietly, eyes closed, her breasts lifting and falling in smooth deep rhythm.

He made no noise, but she sensed his presence beside

the bed. If he touched her—her heart beat high in her throat. The kiss, when it came, was light, a mere brushing of his lips across her forehead. She could not prevent her involuntary movement, but covered it with an indistinct mutter and a rearrangement of her body in the bed.

How long he stood there she had no means of guessing, but her nerves were stretched to the point of pain, when at last the soft sound of the door's closure brought her relief.

Long after that she lay staring into the darkness. What had that strangely tender caress meant? That he thought of her as he did Jenny, someone to be cared for and protected? Or did he now feel sorry for her with her dreams of independence shattered? It did not occur to her that he might have kissed her because he loved her. If it had, she would have dismissed such a stupidity immediately. He had buried his heart with Jenny's mother; she had always known that. Emily had told her and subsequent events had reinforced the truth of it.

Jenny's voice woke her, muffled by the door, yet too clear for Catlin's peace of mind.

'. . . will she stay?'

In answer came Conal's deeper tones, muted and indistinct.

Jenny persisted, 'Yes, but why should she want to go back, Daddy? She's my stepmother and she belongs here with us. She likes being here, she told me she did. You don't want her to go away again, do you, Daddy?'

'No,' Conal answered.

Well, that was clear enough.

'Have you told her? Perhaps she thinks you don't want her, Daddy. Daddy, why did she go before, when I was little?'

Conal asked a question, his voice sharp.

'Gran did. She said Catlin hated living in the city and so she went away, but she doesn't hate living here now, 'cos I asked her. Daddy, will she be sick again today?

She promised me we could go to the zoo after we'd been to see Gran today. Will she be able to go?'

Conal must have suggested she check on Catlin's welfare herself, because the door opened slowly and Jenny's face peeked around it.

'Oh!' she exclaimed. 'Oh, I forgot to knock! Daddy, she's awake. She . . .'

'She is the cat's mother,' Conal rebuked her, but Jenny giggled and flew across the room, launching herself on to the bed and into Catlin's arms with all of the confidence of a much loved child.

'That's what Gran says,' she said comfortably, snuggling beneath the blankets. 'But this is the cat! Catlin, are you well enough to go to the zoo today?'

'Oh, I think so.' Catlin kissed her cheek, then lifted her head to where Conal watched. He was frowning slightly as he came across to sit on the side of the bed.

A finger touched the soft skin beneath her eyes. 'You look a bit smudged there,' he said shrewdly. 'Are you sure you're fit enough to get up?'

'Yes, of course.'

'Not until after breakfast, however. Come on, Jen, we'll show her how well we can make flapjacks.'

This was evidently a high treat. Jenny squealed her pleasure as she hurtled out of the bed and across the room. As her footsteps thundered down the stairs Conal got up, smiling with the cool irony which was so typical of him. 'Don't look so worried,' he mocked. 'I am actually quite a good cook.'

Well, naturally. She couldn't imagine him doing anything badly.

'I'm just surprised that you can do it at all,' she returned stiffly, aware once more of how little she really knew of him.

'Mama believes everyone should be able to care for themselves. Jenny is quite efficient, too.'

She nodded, looking down at the sheet. She knew that her hair was tousled and rough, she wanted nothing more than to get to the bathroom and wash her face and clean her teeth.

'You look as you should look,' said Conal with that uncanny ability to read her mind. 'For the wrong reasons, unfortunately.'

Startled, her glance flew to meet his; he smiled and bent and kissed her, taking his time, using his mouth to push her back into the pillows.

When he lifted his head she was flushed and hot, her expression submissive.

'That's better,' he said, not bothering to hide his satisfaction. 'I spent a very restless night imagining you with your hair tangled across my pillow, your eyes darkened in exhaustion and a few bruises in interesting places on your anatomy.'

His voice was mockingly sensual, but he made no effort to touch her further, merely watched as the colour flowered and ebbed beneath the smooth skin.

'Surely there's a better reason than imagination for spending a restless night?' he suggested smoothly.

Catlin felt a thin film of sweat form across her brow. He was getting to her and he knew it, the glint of amused awareness in the depths of his eyes told her that.

'Have you ever heard of integrity, Conal?' she asked coldly.

He grinned and moved closer, his eyes fixed on the hollow in her throat where a pulse beat rapidly, betraying her reactions.

'What has integrity to do with this?' he taunted, knowing that she was starving for him, that she would go up in flames for him.

'If you had any——'

He laughed, flinging his head back as he did whenever something really amused him. 'Darling, my dearest innocent, you've learnt nothing from all of those men you've slept with, have you? Somebody once said, as I'm sure you're aware, that all's fair in love and war. This, my charming wife, is both. And I have no intention of fighting fair. I'll use any trick I can to get you into my bed.'

She shivered but looked straightly at him, her brows drawn together. 'You don't have to use any tricks,' she said softly. 'You know that.'

For a moment the flicker of flame in his eyes blazed into a conflagration. But seemingly without effort he damped it down.

'Ah, but I want you there permanently,' he said lightly, smiling as if this was a joke, a light flirtation instead of a deadly serious battle. This was her future they were discussing, and he was teasing her with an insolent lack of gravity.

Anger lit the depths of her eyes to gold, brought a flush to lie along her cheekbones. She lifted her arms and drew his head down to hers, kissing him softly, her mouth moving seductively over his in a kiss as provocative as it was gentle.

On either side his hands clenched on to the bedclothes. She could feel the rigidity of his muscles, the tension in his entire body, and knew that he wanted to crush her relaxed softness to him.

Against her lips he said quietly, 'Little temptress. You're asking for trouble.'

His breath in her mouth was so erotic that she trembled, caught in the trap of her own making. Desire sprang into being like a dark flower. Biting her lip, she released him, pressing back into the pillows, but it was too late.

'Oh, no,' he said with a peculiar set smile. The dark head swooped, his mouth crushed hers without gentleness or consideration. For long moments he forced her to accept his superior strength, his hands like clamps of iron on her upper arms as he used his mouth as a weapon in their private war.

At last he lifted his head and stared down into her face, his own coloured by a hard flush. 'And just who was the victor in that battle?' he asked harshly. 'Don't start something you can't finish, Cat. I'm not taking you until you've decided to stay, but I've no objection to picking up what fringe benefits I can along the way to your decision.'

'I hate you,' she said shakily, feeling his heart, heavy and fast, against her own.

He smiled narrowly. 'I know. It's a funny thing, lust, isn't it?'

She shook her head. 'No, it's hell. Let me go, please, Conal. Jenny might come up and get the wrong idea.'

'Wrong idea?' He kissed her gently and then less gently, finally getting to his feet with a wry smile. 'She's an astute child, my daughter. You'll find it difficult to fool her.'

'I don't want to fool her.'

'Just yourself?'

Catlin sighed, turning her head away from the narrowed piercing gaze. 'No,' she said tiredly. 'I just want to get back home and forget this ever happened.'

'Just as you forgot when you last ran away?'

She bit her lip. Well, she had left herself open for that one, telling him that she had modelled herself on the women he fancied, become like those women herself.

'No, this time it's been an exorcism.' In spite of her effort to appear confident she detected that thin betraying note of defiance in her voice.

Conal did, too, smiling down at her with hateful irony. 'There are none so blind ...' he jeered, and laughed at the quick angry look she sent flashing up at him. 'Don't bother to get up. We'll bring a tray up in—oh, twenty minutes.'

'You'll do no such thing. I'm perfectly all right.' Except for the fact that the whole foundation of her life had been cut from beneath her feet.

'Please yourself,' he said, and although he didn't shrug that was what the words conveyed.

So she did, showering and dressing, taming her unruly hair and using make-up to hide the ravages of the night. But make-up couldn't reduce the extra fullness of her lips put there by his cruel kiss, and it was on that that his eyes dwelt when she walked into the kitchen.

She met his mocking glance with as much coolness as she could muster, lifting her chin in a gesture which was as much a betrayal as the pulse beating so rapidly in her ears.

'You always smell so nice,' Jenny sighed, pressing her face against Catlin's hand.

'Fidji,' Conal told her.

Catlin lifted a slim eyebrow. 'Such experience,' she taunted.

'You forget, I bought you your first bottle of the stuff.'

Strangely enough, she had forgotten. For a moment she stared at him, then her gaze shifted and she said, 'Well, you have excellent taste. But that's never been in question.'

'No,' he responded.

He was laughing at her even though his expression was impassive; she turned with what came ominously close to a flounce and began to admire the table setting. Jenny had run outside and picked a bunch of gold and orange nasturtium flowers, set them in a brown pottery vase, squat and glossy in the middle of the table.

'Like sunshine,' said Catlin, touching a flower with a loving forefinger.

Jenny shrugged slightly, but she was pleased at the praise.

Somehow that set the atmosphere for the rest of the day. They ate breakfast in a companionable mood and washed up together, Catlin washing, Jenny drying and Conal putting away.

'We could put them in the dish-washer,' he said, and so they could have, but there weren't all that many dishes and Jenny liked drying.

Catlin should have been surprised that he was so much at home in the kitchen, but nothing about him surprised her now.

Then they tidied the house, which took very little time. Mrs Jansen always left it immaculate on a Friday, ready for the weekend. After that Jenny and Conal swam in the heated waters of the pool while Catlin lay on a lounger in shorts and a skimpy tee-shirt and pretended to read.

'Because she's used to much warmer weather than this,' Conal told Jenny when she asked why Catlin wasn't swimming.

It could have been the reason. As Catlin wasn't telling anyone that she didn't trust herself to frolic semi-naked in the pool with him Jenny was satisfied.

As it was, it took all her self-control not to fix her eyes on him avidly. He was too overwhelmingly masculine, wetness revealing every taut muscle beneath his skin, too overpowering.

It was a relief to go inside and make orange juice in a large pitcher with ice-blocks and mint leaves; not so pleasant to come out again and find Angela and Lee Perrott ensconced in chairs beside the pool with the assurance of old friends.

'Well, hello,' Angela exclaimed in a voice that conveyed, Are you *still* here?

Catlin smiled at her, greeted them both and sent Jenny back into the house for more glasses. Conal had got out of the pool too and had been sitting beside Angela on a wide settee with plump canvas cushions. He rose now, saying casually, 'It's too cold to sit here like this. I'll only be a few minutes.'

Angela smiled up at him. 'We won't go away.'

She really was exceptionally beautiful, Catlin thought dispassionately as she poured drinks—without that aura of sensual allure which Moya possessed in abundance, but the younger woman's skin was flawless and her colouring superb. A little lifeless, perhaps, but she could give Catlin Loring points and still emerge the winner by a very wide margin. A classic cotton shirtwaister set off her classic features and slender curvaceous body. No faded shorts here!

Lee, too, was a handsome creature but with much more life to him than his sister. Too much; Catlin didn't like the way he was eyeing her bare legs. Even if he thought that Conal cared nothing for his estranged wife he was still pushing his luck. Or possibly he just hadn't come up against Conal's possessive streak.

Perhaps Angela too thought he was being too obvious, for she asked, 'You're not cold, Catlin? Surely you're used to a much warmer climate.'

'Slightly warmer, but no one could object to this weather. By and large it's been beautiful since I arrived.' Catlin smiled. 'Beautiful days, beautiful nights.' And her voice lingered on the last phrase as if savouring the memory of those nights.

There was a moment's stiff silence before Angela returned shrilly, 'Yes, it's been a fabulous autumn so far. Sometimes I think autumn is the best season of all, not too hot and no humidity to keep us awake at night.'

She was gabbling. Immediately Catlin felt sorry for her. 'And the winter is not so hard that you need to dread it,' she agreed cheerfully, and began to talk pleasantly of other things which might interest the younger woman. Jenny came back halfway through a discussion on new boutiques and deposited the glasses on the table before arranging herself against Catlin's legs with the air of one who has found their particular niche.

Angela's eyes rested on her, but Conal's return immediately took all of her attention. She glowed up at him, her beautiful face alight with what could only be described as yearning.

Poor kid, Catlin thought, unfortunately catching Lee's amused eyes at that moment. Was this what she would have to put up with if she did lose her head and agree to stay? Always wondering just who had caught his eyes, who had decided that Conal Loring would make the perfect lover, continually watching and waiting for signs of another affair. She must be mad even to consider it!

Not, if one was going to be fair, that one could entirely blame Conal. He was not responsible for the overwhelming impact he made on women, that blend of physical magnetism and mental toughness which was so immensely attractive.

He could, however, stop flirting so skilfully. It wasn't fair; poor little Angela was sitting there with a dazed look in her eyes that reminded Catlin unbearably of herself, six years younger.

Twenty minutes later she was not quite so sympathetic. Angela had spent the intervening time playing an elaborate game, talking to Conal and Lee, even including Jenny, about people and places and occasions which meant nothing to Catlin. It wasn't done with any great subtlety, but Catlin let her go, appreciating the hint of strain in the beautiful dark eyes. Angela was saving face.

Then she said brightly, 'You shouldn't let me run on so, Conal, I know you like my chattering, but it must be very boring to Catlin to hear all about these things she's had nothing to do with.'

'Oh, not very,' Catlin said cheerfully, her voice alight with laughter. 'And it's not as if you were deliberately doing it, is it?'

Lee bent over to poke at something on the flagstones, his shoulders moving slightly. He was laughing. Conal hadn't moved, but from eyes narrowed against the sun his look was bright and piercing.

Stunned by such a direct attack, Angela looked foolish, her mouth slightly open, her eyes wide and startled.

'Nn-no,' she stammered, then gathered her resources and went on more strongly, 'No, of course not.'

But she stopped monopolising the conversation; indeed, as they spoke of books and films and music she was rather subdued and kept shooting furtive little glances at Catlin from beneath her incredible lashes.

They stayed to lunch but left soon after, to watch polo.

'I thought you might be going,' Angela said wistfully.

'Not this time.'

Angela looked even more wistful at his smooth refusal. 'It's a pity you've given up playing,' she sighed. 'You were the best! Do you ride, Catlin?'

Before Catlin could answer her husband's deep voice said calmly, 'Catlin is the best woman I've ever seen on a horse. She grew up in the sheep country of the South Island, Angela.'

'Oh.' The younger woman looked petulant. 'How nice. You'll be able to give Jenny some tips. She needs some, don't you, poor old Jen? If you're going to stay long. Conal are you going to the Marriotts' anniversary party next Saturday?'

'Yes, we're going.'

This drew a startled look from Catlin, who had hoped to be in Australia by then. Jenny's hand, which had been slipped into hers after Angela's sneer, tightened on her fingers.

'Well, we'll see you there, then. Come on, Lee.' And just as if she hadn't been the one to keep him waiting, Angela urged him away.

CHAPTER EIGHT

'SHE THINKS she's so clever,' Jenny said resentfully.

Conal looked at her. 'That's enough!'

Flushed and angry, Jenny protested, 'But she meant me to feel stupid. I'm not a very good rider yet, but I'm not a bad one, either. Why should she be able to say what she likes and not me?'

'Because,' Catlin said swiftly before Conal could speak, 'that's the way things go. Unfair, I know, but young people are expected to be respectful to their elders.'

But Jenny was mutinous. 'Well, I'm not going to expect kids to be respectful to me,' she muttered, 'and I'm not going to pick on kids, either.'

Conal grinned and picked her up, hugging her close to him. 'Believe me, sweetness and light, every kid in the world has said that,' he told her, 'and every grown-up picks just the same.'

Their laughter blended as Jenny nudged her head in her father's chest, bumping him like a young calf. 'I've got the best father,' she cried exultantly, and with a sudden swiftness of perception which was characteristic, 'And the best stepmother too, all goldy and laughing and fun.'

One strong young arm hooked Catlin around the neck; startled, she was tipped slightly off balance so it was easy for Jenny to pull her into her circle. Immediately Conal's arm locked around her too and for long moments they stood together, arms entwined, until Jenny said wistfully, 'Do you think I could have another piece of cheesecake, Catlin dearest? It was *bee-you-ti-full*!'

Laughing, torn by emotions she had never experienced before, Catlin moved free of that too-embracing grip to cut a minuscule slice.

'And that's all, my love. How about helping me to clear the table?'

'O.K.'

They went up to see Emily, but when Catlin made to settle herself in the car Conal opened the door for her, his expression stern.

She looked at him, and then at Jenny.

'Come on,' he said quietly. 'Mama wants to see you.'

In front of Jenny of course she could say nothing, but it was with an irregularly beating heart that she walked with them into the ward.

They stayed for an hour. After an initial penetrating glance Emily had made no acknowledgment of that last meeting, but when it was time to go she said, 'Come again, Catlin.'

She sounded as though she meant it, too. Catlin nodded and smiled and said nothing, but she was bewildered by so abrupt a *volte-face* and could only wonder at what had caused it.

But when Conal told her that he expected her to visit her mother-in-law every afternoon she asked quietly, 'Why?'

'So that you can get to know each other.'

She grimaced. 'I already know her well enough, and I'm sure she doesn't want to get to know me any better either.'

If she had expected him to be angry she was disappointed, because he remained calm but relentless. 'Neither of you has any idea how the other functions.'

'It won't work,' she retorted abruptly. 'We've nothing in common.'

He grinned and reached out to cover her restless hands. 'You have me and Jenny in common. Mama is feeling guilty; she's aware that she's been misjudging you and she wants to make up for it. Is it too much to ask of you, to give her that opportunity?'

'Oh, spare me the histrionics,' she snapped, angry

because he knew too well how to appeal to her compassion.

His fingers tightened on hers. 'Are you going to see her?'

Catlin's lashes flickered as she darted a swift sideways look at him. 'All right,' she answered grudgingly, resenting the ease with which he gained her consent.

'Good.' He let her go and went to change the disc on the stereo. They were sitting in the music room, she reading, he listening to Bach. Patch snuffled several times and twitched, dreaming of who knew what glorious rabbit hunts. It was still warm; apart from one miserable day the weather had been superb ever since Catlin had arrived back.

From beneath her lashes Catlin watched as he moved gracefully from the cabinet which held his enormous collection of records to the stereo. They could have been any family. Jenny was asleep upstairs, but one of her school frocks lay folded neatly on the arm of the sofa. Catlin had just mended a frill. Like any mother, she thought quietly. Complete with dog and handsome, infuriating husband. A T.V. family in lovely surroundings, well-fed, healthy, attractive, rich, intelligent, enviable—oh, there were a multitude of suitable adjectives. And some were correct and some were not.

Conal put on a record, came back to the sofa and as a tenor's brilliantly rich tones surged through the quiet air he smiled and slipped his arm behind her, pulling her gently so that her head came to rest against his shoulder.

She stiffened, but he said, 'Hush, don't be silly,' and she succumbed to her yearning and lay against him, listening as the ravishing, florid music charmed her ears. He had become more demonstrative, touching her with enjoyment, making no secret of his pleasure in her body and her looks, his brilliant gaze openly appreciative. If only she could give in to her love, forget about his women! Day by day she was becoming fonder of Jenny, falling more deeply in love with Conal, picking up the threads of a life she had never expected to enjoy. She knew now that she could be happy here: with Jenny and Jenny's brothers and sisters and a Conal who loved her, even with Emily. She and her mother-in-law would probably never be great friends, but they could probably find some common ground to meet on.

If only . . . if only . . . Unconsciously she sighed.

'Tired?'

'No. Not in the least.'

He moved slightly, turning her head so that his mouth touched her forehead. 'Sad?'

'A little.'

Silence before he said quietly, 'Why not give in, Cat? You know you're beaten. Why not admit it?'

'Because I'm not beaten. Conal, did you look at those papers? The figures for the bookshop, I mean.'

'Yes.' He smoothed a thick silken lock back from his questing lips.

'And——?'

He laughed softly, beneath his breath. 'Oh, it seems a good investment, if that's what you want to do.'

She nodded. 'Ah, well, that is what I want to do.' Obstinacy made her continue, 'I'll have to start saving, I suppose. I just wanted your assurance that I wouldn't have made a mistake if I'd had the money to buy it. I've already written to tell the owner I can't.'

'Catlin.'

'Yes?'

'Are you trying to pick a fight?'

She recognised the silky voice. 'No.'

'Then shut up.'

Which was all very well but got them no further than a very gentle kiss when the tenor had finished pouring his heart out, and a keen, sardonic glance from Conal as she made her excuses and left him to go to bed.

Then the weather broke and for several days there was rain before a high came across the Tasman Sea, bringing with it days of delicious crisp warmth and evenings when it was pleasant but not strictly necessary to light a fire.

Each day Catlin went to see Emily; the hour they spent together was long, but it was not the ordeal Catlin had thought it would be. On the Friday she had to drop the Mercedes into the garage for a check-up and take the bus. She was a little late and Emily was sitting in her chair looking depressed even though she had two other friends visiting her.

They left soon after and Emily said abruptly, 'I've been putting off apologising ever since Conal told me, but I must tell you how sorry I am that I told you about your trust.' She looked weary. 'I wasn't quite sure you knew.'

'Yes, I realised that.'

Emily glanced down at her hands, slightly knotted with arthritis but well cared for and slim still. 'I was wrong about other things too.'

'I doesn't matter,' Catlin said swiftly, surprised to find herself wanting to spare the older woman. Once she would have enjoyed Emily's humiliation. Not now.

'It does, I'm afraid.' Emily's tones were dry. 'Claire was my goddaughter and I loved her as much as if she had been my own child. When she and Conal fell in love I was ecstatic; their marriage and Jenny's birth made me the happiest woman in New Zealand. Then she died and I was shattered, completely broken. In a way, more so than Conal, I think. He grieved for her and then began to recover. I found it impossible. Jenny was a constant reminder of the sweetest girl I'd ever known.'

'And then he married me.'

Emily nodded. 'Yes. You're an intelligent woman, I shouldn't have to spell out why I was so astonished. I still cannot understand why he did it.'

'Nor I,' Catlin answered, meeting honesty with honesty.

'Well, perhaps he saw your potential. I'm sorry I was so unco-operative. I could have spared you some of the misery you went through.'

Catlin's smile was twisted. 'Not much.'

'No. It was Conal, wasn't it?'

'Of course. I was no more immune than any other woman.'

Both women were silent before Emily said, 'A few days ago Conal said you had had to go, that you needed the time to yourself to grow. Was that true?'

'Yes.' Catlin was surprised at his perception, although she shouldn't have been.

'Have you been unhappy?'

Shrugging, Catlin answered, 'No, not once I got over my infatuation. I had too many other things to do.'

'Growing up.'

'That, too.'

Emily smiled. 'It's a pity we didn't all meet for the first time now,' she said deliberately. 'I think we would all have come out of the whole situation better.'

'Probably.'

'Are you going to stay?' As Catlin stood Emily said swiftly, 'No, don't answer that. Conal is the one you should be telling, not me.'

'I've told Conal I'm going.'

'Ah, but he wants you to stay, and what he wants he gets.'

Catlin said coldly, 'Not this time.'

'Good for you!' Incredibly Emily was laughing, real amusement flickering in the blue eyes she had passed on to her son and granddaughter. Catlin stared, and slowly smiled.

'Just don't keep him wondering for too long,' Emily advised 'He has somewhat ruthless methods of resolving a deadlock, my son. Oh,' as the warning bell went, 'if it's of any interest, I intend to move into a unit by myself when Conal—when I'm out of here.'

Catlin sent her a long, level look as she picked up her handbag. 'I imagine both Jenny and Conal will have something to say about that. You are, after all, the only mother Jenny knows.'

Emily looked pleased but said nothing more, merely waved as Catlin left.

On her way into town she was thoughtful, going over those last few minutes in her mind. Unless she was very mistaken Emily had signified her total lack of opposition to Catlin's presence as Conal's wife. Catlin felt rather angry, since he must have discussed her with his mother, but she wondered even more what had made Emily change her mind so drastically.

On impulse she shopped in Queen Street, buying a book for Jenny and a farewell present for Mrs Jansen, a tiny Royal Crown Derby tea strainer and saucer. She had noticed how the housekeeper loved fine china.

Then, still thoughtful, she walked up the street towards the bus stop, and on yet another impulse decided to visit Conal's office and see just who was the owner of the sweet, cold voice which had spoken to her on her first day back.

A very elegant dark-haired woman of forty or so turned out to be the voice's owner; she hid the astonishment Catlin's appearance caused her very well and disappeared into the holy of holies.

Conal came out, smiling, although his eyes were watchful. 'Darling,' he said, and kissed her lightly. 'Come on in. I've another hour or so to do. Would you like to read and have a cup of coffee?'

An hour later they were in the Jaguar heading back across the Harbour Bridge. Catlin said quietly, 'This afternoon your mother gave me permission to resume marital relations.'

'And that's why you're angry?'

The taunting note in his voice re-animated her anger.

'All right,' she said harshly. 'Somehow you've managed to convince your mother that I won't be a dead loss as a wife. Now all that you have to do is convince me that I want to stay.'

His shoulders lifted in a shrug. 'You'll have to do that. I'm not going to force a decision. You'll stay because you want to.'

A car doing well beyond the legal eighty kilometres an hour overtook them, cutting in too close. Against her will Catlin had to admire Conal's driving skill. Without any of the signs of irritation or bad temper that would have been shown by most men he dropped back, allowing the miscreant room.

Catlin hunched her shoulders. It was dusk and the lights along the side of the motorway glowed orange. In a few minutes they would be their normal bright white, illuminating the steady line of traffic heading both ways. More than anything she wanted to tell him that she would stay, but her pride rebelled at being just another of his women. Better to leave with her pride more or less intact.

While she was wondering whether she was fooling herself there was a sound like a rifle-shot. A car mounted the median strip and roared towards them, totally out of control, its headlights expanding enormously. Catlin had time only to gasp before Conal took evasive action; even in the luxurious interior of the Jaguar she was bruised against the seatbelt, flung about as he fought the wheel.

There was a crash, deafening, terrifying, but it was not them. Thanks to Conal's skill they had avoided the runaway monster; it had careered on across, almost making it clear to the other side of the motorway, but on the third lane luck ran out. Now two cars were coupled together in a horrible embrace, someone was screaming, the sound thin and frightening on the warm air.

Conal stamped on the brakes as he brought their car

to a halt. 'Stay here!' he ordered, switching on the four flashing lights.

But Catlin grabbed the torch from the glove box. 'You go and see to them,' she said urgently. 'I'll go back and stop the traffic.'

Just for a moment he hesitated before giving a quick nod.

'O.K. Be careful.'

Surprisingly enough there was little to be careful about. Traffic had already stopped; Conal began organising a clear lane through as Catlin hurried back down the motorway waving the torch up and down.

By that peculiar empathy which occurs in crowds people seemed to know that something was amiss, because already the traffic was slowing. One car stopped. 'Please keep going!' Catlin yelled. 'There's a through lane.'

'My wife's a nurse.'

Catlin gave a quick nod of relief. 'Oh, then about a quarter of a mile ahead. You can just see the warning lights.'

'O.K., my dear. I'd get a bit further off the road if I were you. It's getting darker and you're a bit hard to see.'

She took the suggestion, moving back, and in about another five minutes one of the Land Rovers of Bridge Control came to a halt, beside her.

'O.K., miss, we'll take over. Thank you. Where's your car?'

'Down by the accident.'

'Hop in and we'll give you a ride back.'

By now there was a group of people around the two cars. Within a few seconds a traffic officer came tearing up. Shortly after his arrival Conal detached himself from a group beside an ominous form on the ground and came back towards her. That dreadful screaming had stopped.

'We'd better move on,' he said wearily.

'Won't we have to give the traffic officer details?'

'I've given our name and address. We'll probably have to go in tomorrow, but I'm afraid it's perfectly clear what happened. The poor devil had a blow-out.'

There was blood on his hand, a stain of some sort on his shirt.

Catlin felt sick. 'Is he—are there——'

'One dead, by the look of it—the driver of the car he hit. Two others badly hurt and a couple with minor injuries.'

She handed him her handkerchief. 'Wipe your hand.' And while he did she thought, it could have been us. It could have been him. He could have been killed and I would have had to live for the rest of my life knowing that he was dead.

An ambulance came *whoop-whooping* up the road, followed by another. Conal looked down at her handkerchief, then crammed it into his pocket.

'Come on,' he commanded. 'The sooner we get away the sooner they'll have this lane free for traffic.'

All the way home Catlin watched his hands on the wheel, so strong, so quick to react that he had saved them both tonight. And the thoughts beat through her brain. He could have died. That could be him lying on the cold road, all that magnificent vitality drained and gone, the cold clear brain stilled for ever, the handsome features set in the mask of death.

Tears began to run down her cheeks, silently, unrealised. The thought of a world without Conal was unbearable, an anguish beyond all telling.

Suddenly conscious of her unchecked tears, she sniffed, searching desperately for another handkerchief.

'There are tissues in the glove box,' he said without turning his head. 'You're in shock, don't try to bottle it up.'

'Doesn't anything shock you?'

He smiled without humour. 'Yes, my darling. I don't feel exactly cheerful at the moment, but Jenny will be waiting for us.'

Catlin nodded, scrubbing unmercifully at her face. By dint of convincing herself that she must be able to greet the child with some control she managed to calm down.

Once in the house Conal forced brandy on her, allowed her five minutes with a somewhat sober Jenny and then commanded that she go to bed.

But Catlin changed into slacks and a jersey and made her way quietly down the stairs, impelled by the discovery she had made to find some place where she could be alone.

Outside it was still very warm for autumn. The garden smelt sweet, the last few flowers on the Queen of the Night perfuming the garden with their exotic scent. It was hard to believe that winter was ahead; in the borders the dahlias still held their shaggy heads high, vying for the colour stakes with the delicate vivid nerines, the autumn bulbs and marigolds and chrysanthemums.

Catlin pulled a sky-flower free from the vine and turned it in her hands, gazing down at the pale outline of the bloom.

If she had any sense at all she would pack her bags now and head back to Sydney. At least he couldn't hurt her there.

As she walked down the steps to the beach she knew that she wouldn't. For better or worse the decision had been made for her when that car had come towards them out of the dimness like a wild animal seeking blood. She would stay and take whatever Conal could give her.

It was a quiet evening. The sun had gone down over the Manukau Harbour in a glory of gold and apricot and vivid raspberry light. Now the sky was a delicate pale green with a rosy flush in the east. Against it Rangitoto was black; it should have been sinister, Catlin thought. After all, it was a volcano and as volcanoes went a mere juvenile; there was every chance that it was just biding its time before throwing up another mountain-full of scoria bombs.

But it looked quiet and peaceful and symmetrical, the only accent against its darkness the pale pencil of lighthouse which guided the big ships safely down the channel. Once small baches had shown as pinpricks of light against the pohutukawas which were its main covering. It was a park now and the little baches were getting fewer and fewer. Some day there would be only a wharf and a small pavilion for tourists and a road to the top of the mountain. One of these days she would go there.

There were any number of lights on the other islands. Catlin couldn't remember which was which now and in the half darkness it was hard to distinguish between islands and the mainland, but lights twinkled on Waiheke and Ponui and the Whangaparaoa Peninsula and beyond them were the Noises and Kawau and the Mahurangi Peninsula, Cape Rodney and Great Barrier and Little Barrier and, forming the eastern portal of the harbour, the great bulk of the Coromandel Peninsula with Moehu Mountain as its final sentinel.

And not too far away, in its own private cove overlooking yet another handful of islands, was the Loring bach. Catlin put her hands up to her face for a moment, defying tears to come. The acrid taste of disillusion was still strong in her; it would never go, because she loved him.

A small runabout headed in towards the boat-ramp on Takapuna Beach. Small though it was it was taking no chances. As it came about to straighten up she saw a red lamp change to green. Port and starboard. Port was red, starboard was green. And that was about all that she had learned from the days spent on Conal's great racing yacht. While in Australia she had done plenty of sailing, part of the campaign to prove that she was as capable as Belinda Scargill, who had been able to discuss yachting intelligently. Most of Catlin's experience had been in small boats; if she wanted to she would probably be able to cope with anything he asked her to do on a yacht now.

It suddenly seemed a very petty ambition, to outdo another woman. Head bent, Catlin walked across the soft, dry sand beneath one of the pohutukawa trees and pulled herself up on to a great rough branch, grown especially to sit on, so Jenny had informed her.

Through the canopy of leaves she could see stars, distant pinpoints of light. She sat quietly, her feet tucked up beneath her, one arm slung about the branch, her cheek resting against it.

Silently though he moved she heard him before he saw her. He said nothing, just stood in the cool sand and looked around then came in through the cloak of leaves and sat down on the branch beside her, one leg bent at the knee, the other dangling free. He took her free hand and they sat together for a long time without speaking. He knows, she thought, confusion and happiness inextricably mixed in her heart.

At last he said, 'Made your mind up yet?'

'Yes.' Her voice was so quiet it was almost a whisper, but he heard her.

'And?'

'I'll stay.'

If Conal had shown any signs of satisfaction she would have immediately reversed her decision. Perhaps he realised this, for his voice was calm, without emotion.

'Good.'

'Just one thing. Two, actually.'

'Conditions, Cat?'

She nodded. 'Yes. No more women. And I don't—I'm not ready to go to bed with you.'

He might have been expecting this. 'O.K. You'll get rid of your lover, too.'

'Yes.' Well, it wasn't difficult to cut free from someone who didn't exist.

He sprang down on to the yielding sand and pulled

her gently down. 'We'd better go back. Jenny will wonder what's going on.'

'Yes, I suppose so.'

But before he let her go he bent his head and kissed her without passion. His mouth was kind, his hands gentle on her upper arms, but he held her firmly, refusing to let her pull free.

And when he finally lifted his head it was to say quietly, 'This time we'll make it, Cat. The past can't be forgotten, but in time we'll build happier memories, you and I.' No word of love, but she didn't want him to lie to her.

'And Jenny.'

'Yes.'

He told Jenny the next morning. Predictably she was esctatic, dancing around them like a small dervish before demanding that they go out to celebrate.

'Where to?' Conal looked amused.

'Motat.' At Catlin's bewilderment she elaborated, 'The Museum of Transport and Technology. Oh, Catlin, you'll love it! It's got an old-fashioned sweetshop and neat old cars and fire-engines and they work and you can go around on a tram and——'

Catlin laughed, clapping her hands over her ears. 'O.K., O.K., we'll go!'

'Well, Daddy likes going,' Jenny said ingenuously.

It was fascinating, one of the most enjoyable days that Catlin had spent for a long time.

'Not that you can see it all in one day,' Conal agreed as he bought them delectable potato chips from a stall charmingly disguised to look like one of the old trams.

'Didn't you love the old cars?' Jenny demolished her chips with gusto. 'I like the fire engines the best. Oh, look—there's Joanne and her mother and father!'

She shot off to where a small dark girl hopped impatiently from one foot to another as her parents spoke to each other. Catlin looked up at Conal, smiling, met the blaze of passion in his glance with a greatly increased colour.

'I'm with Mummy and Daddy.' Jenny's clear voice was important. 'Come and say hello.'

They all came; they were nice. Joanne's father was a lawyer and her mother was a potter. Catlin found herself relaxing. When they had gone it occurred to her that she would rather like to have her for a friend.

'Let's go home,' Conal said blandly. 'I'm going to take Catlin out to dinner and she'll need time to prepare herself.'

Surprised, Catlin looked up and met his mocking scrutiny with some confusion.

'Eight o'clock,' he told her firmly.

It was a very pleasant evening. Conal was his most urbane, charming self. They drank champagne and ate the kind of meal Catlin hadn't known existed, and when the car slid quietly into the garage she sighed gently.

'Tired?'

'A little. And full of the most delicious food. And drink.'

His chuckle was definitely amused. 'Just the right mood, in fact, to ring your friend in Sydney and tell her you won't be coming back.'

'Oh, but——'

'Why put it off?'

Well, that was unanswerable, so of course she rang. And it would happen to be the one night when Deb was giving a party. Dry-mouthed, Catlin told her her news. Her reaction was not unexpected.

'Listen!' Deb shouted above the din in the background. 'Listen, Cat, you make sure you know what you're doing. I suppose—will you lot *shut up*! Ah, that's better. I suppose you've been in love with him all the time?'

'Something like that,' Catlin acknowledged.

'And he? How about him?'

Catlin's hesitation told her all she needed to know. 'Oh, you stupid twit, you're going to break your heart all over again!'

The sounds of a scuffle made Catlin look with some astonishment at the receiver. A masculine voice came on. 'Hello, darling. What the hell are you doing over there? Come on home.'

That was Deb's latest, a lanky exquisite with a profoundly patrician accent and the brain of a scientific genius. He did something important in a laboratory somewhere.

Catlin sighed. 'Not now, Garth.'

'But, darling, there's nothing *there* for you, I'm dying of unrequited love here. Leave your shaky little island and come back to me——'

The receiver was jerked from Catlin's hand and Conal spoke into it, his expression icily impassive. He said little, but it was cold, crisp and very much to the point. Catlin stared at him, furiously angry at his interference, and made a grab at the receiver. He caught her hand, holding her still until the annihilated Garth had taken himself away.

'Your friend is back on,' he said, and put the receiver to her ear.

'Catlin?'

'Yes.'

'Cat, what on earth did he say to Garth? He's turned stone cold sober and is shaking away in a corner. Is he a psychopath or something? Cat,' when she didn't answer, 'Cat, I think you'd better come back home.'

'No, everything's fine. A—a misunderstanding.'

Another silence while Deb digested this. 'Oh, did he think—oh, *yes*, I see. Hell, Cat, he's too jealous to be safe!'

'Nonsense.' It was impossible to talk with Conal listening. Catlin lifted her head and glared at him, her eyes golden with rage and frustration. His face didn't change expression and he made no attempt to go, either.

'Listen, Deb, I'll send you my share for the flat. I'll be across in——' she looked at Conal.

'Three weeks,' he said implacably.

'Three weeks, and we'll organise things then. O.K?'

'No, it's not at all O.K.,' Deb retorted darkly. 'But if you really are sure I suppose it will have to be.'

When the receiver went down Catlin burst out, 'How dare you—you had no right to——'

'I had every right to tell your lover where to get off,' he said harshly, grabbing her flailing hands and pinioning them behind her back. 'That's the last time you speak to him. Or I'll make bloody sure neither you nor he care to risk a repetition of what will happen if you do!'

'You don't frighten me,' she stated with a valiant attempt at nonchalance.

He smiled. 'Don't I?' Deep in his eyes a flame grew as he forced her closer to him until the tips of her breasts were just touching his chest. 'You should be afraid,' he said coolly. 'You've agreed to stay with me. I have every right to take you.'

'You promised . . .'

He nodded. 'We both promised, remember? Talking to your boy-friend might have been keeping to the letter of that promise, but hardly to the spirit, was it?' His voice deepened, became infused with contempt, yet in his eyes that flame grew, devouring her. 'I should take you now, and then we'd have no more of this tension and frustration. You want me. Heaven knows I want you.'

Her breath caught in her throat, but she swallowed and said clearly enough, 'You touch me and I'll leave you again. I mean it, Conal.'

'Wherever you went I'd find you.' He smiled again, sliding his hands up her arms to come to rest across her back. 'I'd hunt you down,' he said huskily. 'You'd never feel safe, Catlin, never stop looking behind you. And when I found you I'd show you exactly what that beautiful body was made for, wring the last amount of pleasure from my domination of you, reduce you to a mindless slave to my will.'

Although she shivered, white-faced, defiance still glittered in her gaze. 'You couldn't do it,' she whispered.

'Do you think not?' He sounded amused, so calm as if they were discussing a book both had enjoyed, but there was a dark intensity of passion in his eyes. 'You don't know yet what you're capable of feeling, my darling. The idea of submission fills you with horror, but I promise you it will be a willing capitulation.'

Held captive by the husky, sensual note in his voice, she could say nothing, but what he was threatening her with was the ultimate humiliation. Common sense had no part of this abandonment of body and soul.

She flinched as he lifted her arm and kissed the soft hollow inside her elbow, his mouth moving over the fine skin. Then she jerked back, exclaiming 'No!' in a choked voice, and with one swift, fierce movement of his hands her shirt was ripped and she was revealed in all her shame, the pink tips of her breasts shouting forth their message of arousal.

'See?' he said hatefully.

A deep breath turned into a sob. Catlin brought up a hand curled into a claw and he said, 'Are you ready for me? Because that's what you'll get,' and her hand sank back to pull the remnants of her shirt across her breasts.

'I despise you,' she said thickly.

He nodded. 'I know. Hell, isn't it, wanting someone you despise. I wonder how long you'll last before you beg me to take you.'

'Never. *Never!*'

His mouth closed over hers in a kiss that began as a punishment and ended so seducingly sweet she sagged against him while the blood drummed in her ears. Even when his mouth moved to her breast and took a fiery path to the sensitive nub she could not break away. Her breath came harshly through her lips as she tried to lever herself free, but the hot fire in her loins flamed higher and higher, burning out anything but her need for satiation.

'How soon is never?' he murmured after long minutes, watching with cruel eyes as she turned her head away and pulled her shirt across while her body throbbed and ached for him.

CHAPTER NINE

AT THE Marriotts' there was no sign of Moya Southcott, but Angela was absolutely stunning in white and gold silk which gave her fresh virginal beauty a hint of the temptress. She was very young, Catlin thought judicially, resolving to be forbearing if ill-luck should put them in the same group for any length of time. After all, the girl wasn't to blame for Emily's manipulations, and Conal's attraction was potent enough to send anyone a little off her head.

No sign of Maxie and her Red either. It promised to be a rather boring evening.

That it wasn't was due in a large part to Lee Perrott. He appeared as Catlin was talking to a man who treated her with exaggerated respect, and when her companion turned away hissed, 'They're dancing next door. How about it?'

Involuntarily Catlin's eyes sought her husband. He was talking to a very elegant woman, match-thin and with hair the exact colour of Belinda Scargill's.

'Why not?' she said lightly.

The man she had been talking to smiled and urged them on. Lee chuckled as he escorted her into the next room, and Catlin sent him a questioning glance.

'He wants a favour from Conal,' he explained.

'Poor man!'

He looked at her. They were much of a height and she didn't have to tilt her head to see into his eyes.

'You really mean that, don't you? Soft hearted beneath that rather dragonish exterior.'

'*Dragonish?*' she laughed, relaxing into his arms. 'Oh, come now, Lee . . .'

'Don't you know that Angela is terrified of you? And

Moya Southcott too, in spite of her loud protestations to the contrary! You swept in, took one look at the opposition and without bothering to use any finesse at all disposed of them both.' His grin was openly admiring. 'Rumour has it that Conal has met his match at last. Those who knew you before are scratching their heads and saying nervously that six years certainly has done a lot for you.'

Catlin would have been inhuman not to have felt a warm glow of satisfaction at his words, not in the least tempered by her knowledge that that was exactly the effect he had hoped for.

'Sure you don't want a favour from Conal too?' she asked, laughing, arching her brows at him.

Not at all put out by her recognition of his tactics, he grinned again and swung her into a series of turns which required all her concentration. He was a superb dancer.

'Nope,' he said cheerfully. 'Nary a thing. And if I did I'm definitely going the wrong way about it. He's already given me the kind of deadpan glare that has all his cohorts ducking for cover. A possessive man, your husband.'

She nodded, carefully avoiding the area of the room where intuition told her Conal was standing.

'Very,' she said drily, and almost immediately, without caring about discretion, 'Is Angela very upset? I didn't want her to be hurt.'

'*Very* softhearted! No, in her case it's her pride that's done a tumble, not her heart. And it will be a good thing for her. She'd begun to think that her looks could get her whatever she wanted and was trading on them quite unmercifully.' He shrugged, adding with brotherly candour, 'She even thought she could outdo Moya Southcott at her own game. Well, I'm the first to admit that Angie's a stunner, but Moya is something else again! As even you, my kindhearted, generous Mrs Loring, must admit.'

'Oh, I do.' It hurt to say it, but she managed a suitable light tone. 'A very sexy lady.'

'Well, if Moya couldn't hold Conal, and she couldn't, what the hell hope had Angie? She was living in a fantasy world.' He tightened his hold a little. 'When you appeared out of the blue it was quite obvious just why Conal's been so circumspect these last six years.'

Catlin smiled, not inclined to discuss Conal's love life with this rather startlingly frank man. But she wondered once more if she had misjudged Conal. Maxie had said there were very few names which had been linked with his, and in his own way Lee had borne out her statement.

Something to ponder, but not now. 'You're holding me too close,' she told him sweetly.

'Sorry, pretty lady. You know,' gazing into the clear dark gold depths of her eyes, 'you're not beautiful, but you've certainly got something.'

'The something in this case being a husband,' she retorted. 'Don't flirt with me, Lee. I refuse to play games.'

He lifted his brows at her. 'Frightened of him?'

'Not in the least.' The promptness of her answer startled her.

'Aha, but I think you should be. It's a well known fact in the country that it doesn't pay to cross Conal Loring. He's fair but deadly. Make a mistake and he'll chop you down with a total lack of emotion; try to cheat him and he doesn't rest until you're stripped of everything.'

Something cold shivered across her skin. The music altered tempo, becoming smooth and sweet—music for lovers.

'What do you do, Lee?' she asked.

'I'm a lawyer. A very junior partner, but one day I'll have my own firm. Which is why,' with a flourish which brought them to the edge of the floor, 'I'm relinquishing you to your husband. I don't need favours from him now; I may in future!'

Conal must have been watching them, for as their feet slowed to a stop he was there to greet Lee with a smile which didn't reach his eyes.

To Catlin he said nothing, but his arms were cruel as they enfolded her, hauling her against him in a grasp as sensual as it was painful.

'Hey!' she protested, trying to lighten the inexplicable tension between them. 'This is supposed to be dancing, remember?'

He said nothing, but one hand tugged her head back slightly and when she looked up at him he bent his head and kissed her, lightly, briefly and mercilessly.

'Conal?' she whispered, shocked at such a public display of passion.

'Just in case anyone else gets the idea that they can flirt with you with impunity,' he muttered beneath his breath.

'But——'

'Shut up.'

She shut up, fuming. He had no right to brand her so ostentatiously, force her to accept his public statement of ownership. And just because she had enjoyed a dance with a personable man! Possessiveness was one thing, she thought grimly, but this was an open declaration of mastery, and she did not feel inclined to accept it.

'I can feel resentment shooting out of the top of your head,' he told her, and rested his cheek against the amber silk of her hair. His hands slid slowly to hold her against him, cruelty gone but the strength still there, daring her to object. 'Stop glowering or my status will drop. People will think I'm besotted and unable to control you.'

The note of lazy humour in his voice made her bristle, but she caught an avidly interested look from Angela Perrott and hated herself for responding to it with a totally spurious relaxation.

A feline smile curled her mouth. She tilted her head back and asked sweetly, 'And that would annoy you?'

Hard blue eyes glittered down at her. Oh yes, he was still furious; he just made a better job of hiding it, that was all. 'Not in the least,' he said, watching as colour crawled along her cheekbones. 'Because you know and I know that I only have to kiss you—in a certain way—and touch you—in certain places—and you surrender as abjectly as the most meek Arabian woman to her master.'

In spite of herself—in spite of everything she had learnt about herself in the last six years—something unregenerate and primitive buried deep within her responded to the silky chauvinism of his words. Her mouth trembled as she looked up to meet the passionate darkening of his glance. He smiled and his eyes swept her face and throat, finally coming to rest on the secret hollow between her breasts.

'Because,' he said through lips which barely moved, 'you know that you're mine. When it comes to the crunch, Cat, that delectable body of yours rules both your head and your heart, doesn't it? I've heard often enough that women never forget their first lover. I believe it now. Somehow I imprinted myself on your subconscious, so that although it maddens you to admit it you can't deny me.'

'I could be a nymphomaniac,' she said from between her teeth.

He laughed at that, flinging back his head in appreciative enjoyment before, with a wickedly meaning intonation, saying, 'I do hope so, darling.'

Catlin blushed again, but the inanity of her remark made her writhe with shame. 'Oh, I'd like to see you get your desserts!' she sighed.

'I have. You.'

The music ended then, just in time. Conal kept his arm about her waist as he took her to meet several other people. Some she knew from six years ago; she found herself wondering rather guiltily whether she would ever get over this feeling of smug satisfaction at their obvious astonishment, and decided that she had paid for it. Six years before she had lived in hell; a small triumph was little enough recompense.

Somewhat to her surprise she found she was enjoying herself. They were not ogres after all, merely sophisticated people who had probably been totally at a loss with the shy, ingenuous child she had been then. Now, after that initial astonishment, they revealed themselves as entertaining, even pleasant.

After a while she and Conal became separated again and there was Lee, bold eyes laughing as he brought her a glass of the soda water she asked for.

'Sure? I didn't think anyone actually drank the stuff by itself.'

'It's hot in here and I'm terribly thirsty. Lemonade's too sweet, so soda water it has to be.'

He shrugged. 'Well, each to his own. Now shall we begin again to make Conal jealous?'

'Is that what we're doing? Why?'

'Well, I don't intend to,' he returned lightly. 'I'm just talking to the most interesting woman in the room. Unfortunately Conal seems to find that sufficient reason to make him bristle. Would you like to dance?'

'No, thank you.' She should send him away, but a glance at his audacious countenance was enough to confirm that he wouldn't go. Whether it was just mischief or not, he fully intended to stay close to her whenever Conal moved away.

'So,' he said deliberately, 'tell me what you think of those pioneers who introduced British birds here?'

Catlin choked with laughter and surprise, eyes alight with amusement, and began to tell him just what she thought of those sadly misjudged forefathers. It soon developed into a serious discussion; for about ten minutes they argued amiably before Lee looked up and greeted Conal with just enough mockery in his voice and expression to set every nerve in Catlin's body tingling. For some reason Lee was intent on goading Conal, and she, stupidly, had played into his hands.

It was Conal who told her why, his voice cold and indifferent as he drove them home at two o'clock in the morning after some of the most difficult hours Catlin had ever spent.

'Moya was going round with him,' he said with an icy dispassion. 'So don't, my dear, think he's about to fall in love with you. He's merely doing his best to make me look a fool.'

She sighed wearily. 'I suppose you stole her from him.'

'She's hardly a piece of plunder, but that's probably how he would put it.' Something insinuated itself into the deep cold voice, the hint of a sneer. 'Disappointed, darling?'

'Don't be an idiot.'

She leaned back against the headrest. He had behaved abominably after breaking up that second interlude, holding Catlin's hand, acting like a devoted lover who could barely keep his hands off her, while all the time his blue eyes blazed with condemnation and anger and around them people smiled and sent each other significant looks.

Now her nerves were stretched like piano wires and she was braced for one of the ferocious battles she remembered.

Conal said no more, however, treating her with an aloof courtesy that made her furious and them sombre. She refused his offer of a nightcap and slipped away up the stairs to bed, lying there waiting for him to come in and begin denouncing her with the cold cutting restraint which had always reduced her to silence and fear.

But he didn't come—at least not until five hours later, when he and Jenny ruthlessly hauled her out of bed, ignoring with identical callousness her protests and feeble attempts to stay beneath the covers.

'Go away!' she moaned. 'I've got a headache and it's the middle of the night.'

'It's seven in the morning and you drank soda-water, so you haven't a hangover.' Conal turned to his daughter, 'Darling, go and get poor Cat an aspirin, will you?'

Jenny giggled and disappeared.

'What the hell is going on?' Catlin demanded. 'It's Saturday, and I don't have to get up at seven.'

'Yes, you do, darling. Jenny is spending the day with Joanne and you and I are going sailing.'

'Sailing?' Catlin sat on the side of the bed, and stared at him with intense suspicion while her heart swelled. He was laughing down at her, very sure of himself, big and masculine and virile in shorts and a cotton shirt, his gaze roaming her tumbled abandon with sensuous appreciation.

'Nothing better for a headache,' he said now, turning as Jenny came carefully back into the room.

'But doesn't Jenny want to come too?' Catlin didn't want to spend time alone with him in the crowded confines of a yacht, however large.

Father and daughter exchanged complicated glances.

'No,' Conal said lightly. 'Apparently she and Joanne have something planned for today; she just didn't think to let us know before. Right, on your feet, lady. Breakfast is ready and we leave in half an hour.'

Which they did, and left Westhaven shortly after that, the *Islander* responding like the thoroughbred she was to Conal's hand at the helm as he negotiated the inner Harbour and took her round North Head.

Soon the freshening wind drove Catlin below to find a jersey and she explored an enormous hamper of food, far too much for a day out. Suspicion hardened into certainty; she climbed back up the companionway and accused Conal of hijacking her before her head had got through the hatch.

'That's right,' he said cheerfully.

She gasped and stared at him. 'For how long?'

'At least four days.'

'Are you mad?'

He grinned at her. 'Not in the least, my darling.'

'But—Jenny——'

'Is enjoying very much the prospect of a long weekend with Joanne and her parents.'

Catlin collapsed on to the top step of the companionway. 'My clothes,' she said. 'I haven't any clothes.'

'Mrs Jansen packed a suitcase. Not,' he added calmly, 'that you'll be needing many.'

Heat scorched its way along her veins. He had no right to look at her with such deliberate, open desire, as though she were a slave woman used for one purpose.

'*Why?* You said——'

'I said a lot of rubbish.' His mouth tightened. 'After last night's little episode I decided that I'd waited long enough.'

'You—you've organised all this since last night?' Her voice rose shrilly against the soft slap, slap of the waves against the hull.

'Yes; I'm not having any more conjecture, or any more idiots like Lee Perrott trying to make up to you. When you come back from this weekend you're going to be quite clearly and distinctly mine.' Again that bold, raking stare. 'A woman with so much to handle that there's no way she could cope with any more. If you want a lover, Cat, you can have me. I may not be the one you dream about, but, when you're awake you won't be thinking of anyone else but me.'

There was no answer to that. And if the truth be known, wasn't that what she had wanted? To have the decision taken from her hands, to save her pride. Perhaps that was what had prompted her reaction to Lee's mild flirtation last night.

But she lifted her head and said coldly, 'You promised you wouldn't force me.'

'I have no intention of forcing you.' His smile was very light, very confident. 'If it makes you feel any better shall I promise not to take you until after you've begged me for the third time?'

'No!' She hid her brilliant cheeks with her hands, clamping her eyes shut.

'Only because you know damned well I could make you,' Conal retorted brusquely. 'Haul in the jib sheet, will you? Can't you see the sail's not setting right?'

This she remembered. Fuming, her eyes averted, she reached over and wound in the sheet. Big though the *Islander* was, she had been especially geared to make her simple to sail.

Without acknowledging her expertise Conal asked, 'Think you could put the kite up? No? Take over, then, will you, while I get it ready.'

It was pleasant—correction, she thought stormily—in any other circumstances it would have been pleasant to take the helm of such a magnificent yacht while Conal hauled out the enormous vari-coloured spinnaker and went about organising its hoisting.

So angry was she that the brilliance of the day was entirely lost on her. She even forgot any qualms she might have felt at crewing; any apprehension was bound up with the fear that his disclosure had aroused in her.

How dared he calmly abduct her with the sole intention of making love to her! More than she could handle, indeed! Her scorching gaze raked him as he moved lithely about. How she loathed him! Conceited, arrogant, ruthless swine of a man.

It took a little longer for the two of them to put up the spinnaker, but when it was done Conal sat down in the cockpit shaking his head as she offered him the wheel.

'No, you're clearly capable of managing her.' He leaned back and closed his eyes. 'Call me if you see a whale.'

Gnawing her bottom lip, she watched him uncertainly until a protesting yaw brought her attention back to where it should have been.

'Conal——' she began, only to have him interrupt crisply.

'I didn't get much sleep last night, Cat. Leave it, there's a good girl, until we arrive.'

'But where——?'

He grinned and opened his eyes a fraction. 'Wait and see, darling.'

Beneath the thick fringe of his lashes his eyes were very bright. Catlin hesitated, then shrugged. There was nothing she could do to talk sense into him.

If that was really what she wanted to do. As he apparently dozed and she concentrated on her course she became conscious of butterflies, several flocks of them, beating in her stomach. Suppose he was disappointed in her? He would be expecting an experienced woman, not a near-virgin, if there was such a thing. And could she relax and love him at all knowing that this was yet another example of his possessiveness, that he did not love her?

'Stop worrying,' he advised lazily, startling her. 'Would you like something to drink?'

'I—yes.'

He grinned and went below, reappearing a few minutes later with coffee. While they drank he began to ask her about her sailing experience in Australia; she followed his lead, managing to quell a few of the butterflies, but when he took her mug their fingers touched and she jerked away.

His eyes glittered, but he said nothing.

Soon a couple of ominous flaps forced the decision to drop the spinnaker. They began to tack up the coast. Catlin handed over the wheel and sat quietly, knees up and her arms around them, watching as great flocks of kahawai birds swooped and whirled in search of their prey in the sea beneath. Once a tiny blue penguin surfaced a few metres away and gave them one startled look before diving once more beneath the waves.

Catlin laughed softly, very conscious of her husband's

eyes. It was to be her last purely enjoyable moment for a long time. As they had made their way up the coast a suspicion burgeoned in her mind; stupidly, perhaps, she had thought that they would spend the weekend on the *Islander*. But it seemed that she was incorrect; each tack brought them closer to that one particular headland which hid one particular bay.

Sure enough, when they rounded it Conal said calmly, 'If you'll take her in, Cat, I'll get the sails down.'

White-faced, her eyes cold and dull as pebbles, she said huskily, 'I'll never forgive you for this.'

He shrugged. 'As you wish.'

Numbly she took the yacht in well clear of the reef which provided such good shelter. There was a rattle as they went about, then the mainsail came down and they were ghosting along under the jib towards the jetty. The bay was almost circular, with three small sandy coves bitten out, only one of which had a building in it. The last time she had seen it was when she had brought the car down the narrow, precipitous track from the road and watched for several horror-stricken moments while Belinda Scargill pulled Conal down to her on the big bed in the main bedroom.

As they readied the yacht for mooring Conal remarked conversationally, 'I never saw her again after that weekend.'

'What?'

'Belinda. She went to England, I believe, and married well.'

'Good for her!'

The bitter words hung in the cool sparkling air. He said nothing more but kept an unobtrusive eye on her.

'You needn't worry,' she said. 'I'm not going to run away. I've learnt my lesson.'

'Which is?'

'That running away solves nothing if you leave the problem behind.'

'Ah, but it bought you time. You're better equipped to deal with it, now, aren't you?' As she came up the companionway with a hamper of food he tipped her chin and looked down at her with a quizzical smile. 'All you have to do now is decide exactly what the problem is,' he said, and bent his head to press his lips to hers, ignoring her stiff withdrawal.

The bach was clean and airy, the windows wide open.

'Good,' Conal murmured, 'I asked Heather Turner, who lives with her husband on the farm, to check it out. Put the food away, will you, while I bring the rest of the gear in.'

The trip up the coast had been quick; it was only just afternoon. As Catlin transferred food from hampers into the fridge and an enormous pantry she found herself dry-mouthed, wondering whether he expected her to fall into his arms like a long-lost lover, palpitating with desire.

So much the worse for him. He must know that he was going to have a fight on his hands; arrogant and self-confident though he was, she had never thought conceit a part of his character. It wasn't, of course. He knew his own worth, but he certainly didn't over-value himself.

He intended to use that driving animal attraction between them to force her into his arms. And, she owned candidly, he had a better than average chance of succeeding. Ever since she had come back he had been whittling away at her defences, forcing her to make a reassessment of her very basis for living. She had had to run away; by taking control of her own life she had made a mature woman of herself. If she had stayed in the poisonous atmosphere of their marriage she would have died inside. Her decision to flee had been the correct one, the only one to make.

What she hadn't realised was that she had based that new life on a lie. She had thought her love had turned into hatred, not appreciating that love denied and derided can assume the face of hatred yet still keep its integrity. For six years a determination to prove Conal wrong in his evaluation of her had urged her on so that she used her accomplishments as scores in a game where she was both winner and loser. Conal had been right to force her to come back, for only by returning could she face the implications of what she had done and what she had become.

And so, fighting a rearguard action, she had been forced to confront the truth. His violation of her had begun as that, a violation, but sheer sexual antagonism had been transmuted into desire and the harsh brutality of his lust was transformed into a sweet, tender passion. And she had responded, incandescent, aflame with a matching passion, until the pain of her initiation had brought her down to earth with a thud, sickened and frightened by the intensity of her response. It was that which had sent her stumbling back into her own room; to the young Catlin such an unequivocal response had meant that she was abnormal. What she had learned of the relations between men and women had been culled from books; this confrontation with her own heated sexuality terrified and repelled her.

And of course there had been her fury at Conal's infidelity, the searing sense of inferiority which Emily had inculcated in her; oh yes, she had been very wise to leave. Had she stayed, even as his wife, she ran the risk of submerging her fragile, still-emerging personality in the formed, decisive arrogance of his.

And now? As she set the table for lunch she looked through the window at him, moving about on the *Islander*. No, there was no reason for her to worry about losing her sense of individuality. The independence of the years away had seen to that. What she had to worry about now was whether she could cope with his inclination to unfaithfulness. For the first time ever she wished her relationship with Emily was closer. Not that Emily would know—or tell her—whether he had found it necessary to seek other diversions during that brief first marriage.

Catlin set pâté down, frowning. It didn't matter, anyway. Claire he had loved, and he most definitely did not love Catlin. Could they possibly build any sort of satisfactory relationship on the basis of practicality and lust on his side and this damned, nagging love on hers? It was clear that he thought so. But the answer must come from her. And even as she pondered on it she knew the answer. Had known it, in fact, ever since that runaway car menaced their safety. It was better for her to live with Conal than to go through life alone.

She could only hope that this love of hers, so painfully conceived, and brutally used, would be some compensation for the anguish that such a one-sided relationship would inevitably bring. A woman's place in life, she thought wryly, to give and give of herself and receive only crumbs in return.

Still, at least she could make sure he found it worthwhile to stay close to her bed. And, she decided with a recklessness she rather enjoyed, with any luck he might find it too exhausting to be unfaithful!

'Something seems to be amusing.'

She looked up, startled, and for one moment her breath caught in her throat. He was magnificent, tall and tanned, exuding virility, and his smile had a lazy, waiting quality to it that should have warned her. Delicate colour touched her cheeks.

'Graveyard humour,' she said.

He grinned and reached for her. Holding her securely against him, he bent his head and murmured into her temple, 'I like it when you smile to yourself. You were doing it at the hotel, remember. I came in through the door and you had that tantalising, mocking smile as you watched someone across the room. I knew then that I had to have you.'

'You were an absolute swine!'

'Mmm.' He laughed as his teeth met on the soft lobe

of her ear. His breath tickled erotically. 'I know. And you were a complete tease. You returned everything you got with interest. It took me all my time not to go up to your room with you and dispense with the preliminaries. I thanked God for the impulse that had made me demand to see you.'

'Dispense with what preliminaries?' Catlin jerked her head away from his caresses and stared up into his mocking eyes, her own snapping with outrage. 'What do you mean, dispense with the preliminaries? Preliminaries to what?'

He laughed and kissed her, letting her feel his strength. 'This,' he said against her lips. 'If there's one thing I've been certain of all along—and I don't mind telling you it's the *only* thing I've been sure of—it's that we'd end up as lovers. You snarled very prettily at me, my darling, but you were extremely conscious of me. Just as I was of you. Whenever we were together sparks flew.'

'And you are so experienced——'

'Sh!' He touched her mouth with his finger, replaced it for long enjoyable moments with his mouth. 'Let's make a pact, shall we? If you don't refer to my affairs I'll try not to be jealous of yours.'

'Jealous?'

Something gleamed beneath the heavy lashes. 'Jealous,' he said smoothly. 'As in murderous. Let's forget it, shall we? Lunch ready?'

She nodded.

'Good. I'll just wash my hands.'

CHAPTER TEN

THEY DRANK half a bottle of wine with lunch and then went for a walk along the cove, climbing the cliff at the end to sit on the short grass and gaze out to sea. The sun and a late night combined with the wine made Catlin sleepy; she yawned twice and Conal stood up, hauling her with him.

'Come on, back to the beach. You can have a sleep there.'

There was no undertone to his voice, nothing to make her wary, but she couldn't prevent a quick sideways glance. He looked sombre, the handsome mask of his features successfully hiding his thoughts.

Regretting it already?

A small sigh, instantly suppressed, escaped her. Just who did she think she was, hoping to tame him? Other, far more beautiful women had tried and failed. The only things she had to offer him were the love she still resented and the sexual attraction which time would probably diminish.

The sand beneath her feet was hard and smooth, wave-rippled. The bach stood above the cove, up a rise covered in coarse marram grass and the tufty silver spines of hare's tails.

Catlin swallowed nervously. The bach seemed to leer at her, the enormous bed in the main bedroom loomed in her imagination. That room had been redecorated since her last visit; Emily's hand was conspicuous by its absence. The furniture was spare and plain, modern yet elegant. Had the bed been changed too, or was it the same one?

'I can't,' she said suddenly, and before Conal could touch her she began to run, panic driving everything from her mind but the basic instinct to flee.

He waited until her headlong rush took her to the soft sward at the foot of the rise, then tipped her off balance by the simple expedient of thrusting his foot between hers. She fell, winding herself and sat up, clutching her stomach, swaying back and forth as she gasped for breath.

'Yes, you can,' he said, and came down beside her.

As she regained her breath she realised that he had removed his shirt and thrown it on the ground. He loomed between her and the sun, enormous, threatening, his bronzed shoulders flexed ready to subdue her.

'Please, Conal,' she whispered, hating herself for the note of hysteria in her voice 'I don't want——'

'But I do want.' He came down beside her, his features inflexible with determination, strange, leaping lights in his eyes as they devoured her white, frightened face. 'Oh, yes, I want,' he groaned, reaching for her.

She fought like a wildcat, clawing at him with all of her strength, until he bared his teeth in grim pleasure and slowly, expertly, stripped her, not caring when buttons tore and seams gaped until she was lying panting, sobbing, in nothing more than her cotton briefs.

'Why?' he asked, his eyes on hers, compelling an answer 'Why do you force me to take you? Do you like being raped?'

'No.' Catlin shook her head miserably and wiped her eyes with the back of her hand. 'I'm frightened,' she said before she had time to think.

There was an odd silence. 'Why?' he asked once more. 'I won't hurt you again, I promise, Cat. Is that it, the hidden fear?' and when she didn't answer because she couldn't he bent his head and kissed her gently. 'Trust me,' he said softly. 'The only way you're going to get rid of that illogical fear is to accept me. Let me show you that with me too it can be enjoyable.'

His voice had dropped several tones. She closed her eyes, afraid that he would see the truth in them and turned her head. Her mouth grazed his shoulder. Such a tiny accidental caress, yet he trembled at it. His mouth dropped to the hollow in her throat and lingered there while his hands slid beneath her shoulders, holding her slightly away from the soft ground. His face was damp against her skin.

For long moments they lay clasped loosely together, until the panic which had fuelled her futile flight faded and she brought up her hand to touch the smooth hardness of his shoulders and back. It gave her a fierce pleasure to feel the shock her touch gave him; it was like an electric charge running through his body. Deep within her that treacherous desire stirred. Never before had she indulged her own repressed sensuality. Instinct told her that this was the right and proper occasion. Whatever Conal thought, for her this would be the first time.

His mouth moved slowly over her shoulders, warm, tantalising. He knew that she wanted more, but he made her wait until, tormented beyond endurance by the sudden fierce demands of her body, she guided his head to her breast.

'What do you want?' he asked.

'Kiss me,' she whispered.

'Where? Here—or here?' his mouth made forays.

'You know. Please—Conal——'

He laughed as he began an erotic exploration of her body, using hands and mouth to drive her to a fever of response, her hands shaking as they moved to the buckle of his denim shorts.

This time she was not frightened by her headlong response to his lovemaking. Almost angrily she let down every barrier her adolescent self had erected between mind and body, openly adoring his strength, whispering love words as she allowed her passion free rein.

Conal was as shaken as she by the intensity of her desire, smiling until the triumph she no longer denied him faded into a sensuality as profound as hers. When his hands at last moved to remove the last barrier to his possession she shivered with anticipation, watching him with open delight as he brought himself over her, his thigh parting hers.

But although he lowered himself so that she felt his urgent desire he did no more, his expression set in harsh lines of self-control.

'What—what's wrong?' she whispered, fear almost casting out passion.

'Three times,' he said, and smiled. 'Remember? You have to ask me three times before I'll take you.'

It made her laugh now, relief and desire mixed into an explosive combination. She touched her lips to his shoulder and bit him, hard.

'Please take me,' she whispered. And again, 'Please take me.'

But the third time she stayed silent.

'Temptress,' he groaned, his body hardening beneath the tormenting movement of her hands from shoulder to the tight muscles of his buttocks. 'Ask me, damn you!'

She laughed and moved sinuously beneath him.

'Cat!' His mouth crushed hers, his body tautened in a kind of agony, and then all thoughts of speech were lost in an explosion of passion as they merged into the one ultimate union, breath mingled with breath, his driving energy demanding a like response from her, arms locked about each other as she took him completely into her in a consummation as ferocious as it was satisfying.

Spent, exhausted by the storm of passion that had overtaken them, they lay clasped together, Catlin accepting his weight gratefully until at last he turned his head and kissed her, softly, gently, as though he loved her.

'You are a lady of very special talents,' he said, and rolled over and pulled her to rest against his shoulder.

It was not the sort of remark she had hoped to hear him make, but she accepted it. He was her fate, and whatever happened now must be accepted.

'So are you.'

She could hear the smile in his voice. 'I had no intention of making love al fresco, but it has its subtle delights. Convinced now that I'll never hurt you again?'

Not physically, anyway. 'Mmm,' she murmured, revelling in the warmth of the sun against her naked body. She felt tired, as though she had run an exhausting race, every muscle loosely relaxed. A yawn made her shake.

Conal laughed and pulled her closer, speaking into her hair.

'Well, that was worth waiting six years for!'

'Waiting? Oh, come now, Conal——'

'Waiting,' he interrupted deliberately 'Six years, four months, to be exact. I always wanted you—from the first time I saw you. Do you remember? I'd come to look Mount Fay over before deciding whether or not to buy it and your father gave me a drink. We were out on the verandah and you came galloping up from the river flats on a dun-coloured horse.'

'Yes, I remember.' Catlin turned away from him so that he could see only her back, sun-kissed and smooth against the crushed grass.

Conal bent his head and bit the fine skin very gently, his breath warm. 'How beautiful you are,' he murmured, resting his cheek against her. 'You were beautiful then, lithe and free and laughing but oh, so young! So I put any ideas about you firmly out of my head. Then your father had that heart attack.'

She nodded, tracing a pattern in the sand. His mouth against her back was warmly sensuous. Shivering, she was racked by a resurgence of passion.

'Yes,' he said quietly, sliding his hand between her

breasts to rest against her heart, 'it's always been there, my darling. That's why I was so cruel to you. After we were married I knew I had to keep my distance——'

'But *why*?' she demanded, staring out across the bay.

'I was—I expected you to—to consummate our marriage. I didn't know—I thought it must be that you were repelled by me.'

'*Repelled?*' He laughed between his teeth as his hands became suddenly fierce. He turned her on to her back, holding her still, those cold eyes blazing as they swept her face and body. 'Cat, use your common sense! How could I take you to bed? You were seventeen, a baby, totally innocent and unaware——'

'Oh, *Conal*, you fool! Not so innocent that I didn't know the facts of life. Oh, I wasn't in love with you, I know now that it was only infatuation, but believe me, I wanted you.' She smiled very tenderly at him, smoothing back a lock of dark hair. 'I was poised on the brink of falling in love. My darling, I ached for you, wove fantasies about your prowess as a lover, wanted so hard to grow up so that I could learn how to seduce you!'

It was very quiet. He lay still, staring at her as if she lied to him, his features tensed. 'You were terrified of me,' he insisted. 'I could see it in your eyes every time I came near you!'

'Because you were so remote, so indifferent. You froze me.'

Suddenly he groaned, the proud dark head drooping on to her breast, resting there as she touched his cheek and hair. 'What a bloody fool I was!' he muttered thickly. 'All that self-control wasted!'

'No. I wasn't fit to be a wife to you then.' She touched his mouth, felt it move into a kiss against her fingers. 'It's better this way, Conal.'

'Just like that. All the pain and the grief, all my duplicity, my arrogance and my violence forgotten?'

'Not forgotten.' Incredulity held her silent for a

moment. There had been that in his manner, in the torment of his voice and the anguish she could see in his eyes which revealed the truth to her. Hope long denied burst into flower, irradiating her face. 'Do you love me, Conal?' she whispered, almost afraid to accept what was now so clear.

He moved swiftly, covering her with his body as he kissed her, not fiercely but with a desperation that revealed the depths of his emotions more clearly than any words could.

'Oh, I love you,' he said into her mouth, his voice ragged. 'I don't know when it happened, but I know when I realised it. I came in through the door in that hotel and you were smiling, watching someone, with your lashes lowered and your face turned a little away from me. It was like being hit on the head with a mallet. For a moment I literally couldn't breathe. I thought, so that's it. I felt as though I'd come home after a long journey. I knew then why I'd never divorced you, why I'd insisted you come back. And why no mistress had ever given me more than temporary relief.'

Catlin stiffened, turning a white face away from him.

He rested his hand against her cheek, speaking quickly, with determination. 'Please listen, my heart. I'm trying to be as honest as I can with you.'

After a moment she nodded and he kissed her cheek, and then his eyes closed before resuming, 'So I made you come home with me and I quite shamelessly used every circumstance I could to keep you there while I set out to court you.' His mouth savoured the warm softness of her throat as he slid his arms beneath her back and held her closer, watching every fleeting expression of her face with eager eyes. 'Then I discovered that you couldn't bear me to touch you. It was a very salutary shock to my ego. I didn't know how to cope.'

Smiling rather teasingly she opened her eyes to peep beneath her lashes at his strong face. 'Even though you had your suspicions about exactly what frightened me? You were right, of course. It wasn't you, it was because I was terrified of giving myself away. Every instinct of self-preservation I possess was screaming that if I wasn't careful I'd tumble headlong back into love with you, and I'd been so hurt before ... When I left you I vowed I wasn't ever going to allow myself to become dependent again on a man for my happiness.'

'Darling,' he whispered. 'Oh, my darling, I'd give anything to be able to wipe out the past. The horror in your face when I took you has haunted me ever since.'

The memory brought a sigh to her lips. Immediately Conal let her go, moving to lie beside her, his arm curved comfortingly beneath her shoulders.

'You were right then, too,' she admitted after a struggle with herself. Only complete honesty could ease those excoriating memories. 'It may have started off as a rape, but by the time——' she stopped precipitately, coloured and hid her face in the hard warmth of his shoulder.

'By the time . . .' he prompted, only half teasing.

Her laughter was muffled against his skin. 'I've never admitted it, not even properly to myself until this minute, but of course I was just as aroused as you. I wanted you, quite desperately. It *was* just bad luck that for me the first time hurt so much.'

'Nevertheless, on that first time you had the right to be taken in love instead of anger and lust,' he said with sombre precision. 'Then I could have comforted you, held you in my arms until you slept and reassured you that it wouldn't happen again, that you were unlucky. And my damned lack of sensitivity didn't help, either. There would have been no humiliation to force you into running away. Or taking lovers just to prove that you could be as desirable as Belinda.' He sighed, his arm tightening as his other hand stroked, very tenderly, her shoulder and breast and the lovely curve from hip to thigh.

Catlin had thought that desire so fiercely sated must die; she discovered her mistake now. Beneath the almost absentminded caress of his fingers her skin tightened, grew hot while that knot deep within her began to expand. Her breath grew fast and shallow, coming in soft pants between her lips.

'The only plea I can offer in mitigation is that if I hadn't wanted you so much I'd never have allowed my frustration and despair to drive me into a—well, an explosion like that. I brought Belinda here that weekend quite coldbloodedly to ease my frustration. What made me so furious with you was that experienced and sensuous as she was, I had to pretend that she was you before I could make love. I despised myself. I think I hated you for putting me in such a position, otherwise I wouldn't have reacted so violently that evening.'

The lovely sensations engendered by his hands dissolved as a lightning-shaft of jealousy ripped through her, tautening her body into a bow of rejection. Like stills from a movie came her memories, those red-tipped fingers sliding slowly over the tawny muscles of his back, the husky note of passion in Belinda's voice as she had called him her darling.

'I don't want to hear about it!' she exclaimed harshly, pushing at him, her face pinched and pale.

Conal caught her hands and held them between her breasts. 'We must,' he said deliberately, holding her tormented gaze with his until she stilled and lay quiescent. 'Just this once and then no more, I promise you.'

But he was silent for a moment, frowning as though he found it difficult to choose the correct words. 'I don't know if you realise how frustrating it is for the average man to live in very close contact with a woman legally his, whom he wants, in your own words, quite desperately, and whom he daren't touch. One of the reasons I made love to Belinda was because I was terrified that I'd lose control and take you before you were ready. And because it seemed as though you never would be ready. You had retreated from being that vital, glorious child I'd first seen into a state of blank-eyed hopeless apathy where no one could reach you. I did try, Cat, but whenever I came near you you flinched away from me as if I'd suddenly grown horns and hooves.'

She sighed, admitting the accuracy of his statement. 'I told Deb that it was culture shock, and I think I was right. I thought your—your refusal to consummate our marriage was indifference and rejection. And I was so ill equipped to be anything like the person you needed! Your mother told me about your first wife, you see, and I felt so inferior. I knew I couldn't hope to compete.'

He nodded, his lips forming into a straight line. 'Yes. My mother didn't make any attempt to help. She thought I'd run mad, of course, marrying you. I didn't feel like confiding to her that every time I saw you I wanted to rush you off to the nearest bed. And I had to have her here to look after Jenny. It would have been too cruel to have sent her away.'

'Of course it would have been.' Catlin smiled and imprisoned his hand against her cheek. 'I couldn't have looked after Jenny. I could barely look after myself.'

'Mmm.' Conal bent his head and kissed her throat, then lay back against the sun-warmed grass, pulling her on to him. 'I thought you were like one of your beloved mountain lilies, almost too delicate to transplant to the coast.'

Up by the house a slight wind ruffled the topmost branch of a tamarisk, then died away. As always in the heat of the afternoon the sounds of the natural world stilled; even the cricket that lived under a flagstone in the terrace was quiet. One of the tiny blue and brown butterflies which danced so gaily through the summer and autumn rested a moment on Catlin's shoulder before resuming its search for nectar. The great hibiscus at the end of the terrace held its enormous elaborate flowers up to the sun. They looked, Catlin decided hazily, like magnificent Edwardian hats, all silk and ruffles and pure, distilled colour. Very Merry Widow.

'Tired?'

She had yawned. 'Yes. This making love in the middle of the day is a bad thing. I feel as though I could sleep all afternoon.'

'Why not?' Conal looked wickedly down at her, touching her hot cheeks with a caressing finger. 'We've nothing else we have to do.'

He got to his feet, a magnificent animal, and picked her up, holding her with sensuous enjoyment.

'The clothes,' she said, flushed and very bright-eyed.

'I'll get them later.'

He carried her straight into the shower. Never before had it occurred to Catlin that a shower could be an erotic experience. She discovered it with an exultant surge of passion that met and matched his.

Their second coming together was slower, less reckless, Conal's lovemaking so seducingly sweet that this time she wept and drifted off to sleep on the big bed locked in his arms as he murmured his love, absolute and undying, comforting her as she had never been comforted before.

When she woke it was almost dark and she lay bewildered, wondering where she was. Then memory came flooding back and she smiled, a secret smile, and stretched pleasurably, easing muscles that ached and noting with unsurprised eyes several incipient bruises. Conal was a tender lover, but when his passion had overridden his self-command he had been unable to control his great strength.

It was, she thought dreamily, rather flattering to know that she had the power to overturn the self-restraint that cold, clever mind normally exercised. Flattering and a great responsibility. One she had every intention of living up to.

Sounds from the kitchen made her leap to her feet and snatch some clothes. In the heat of the day her nakedness had not mattered, but this was autumn after all, and although at some stage of her sleep Conal had pulled up the duvet to cover her the air was cool on her bare shoulders and arms.

Ten minutes later, clothed and just a little shy, she walked into the kitchen.

'Hello,' he said, smiling at her with a teasing charm that told her that he knew exactly how she was feeling.

She gave a little laugh and pressed her hands to her hot cheeks. 'Don't make me blush!'

'I'll be rather sorry when I can't. I like that reddy colour. I've got everything ready for a Chinese meal. Would you like a drink before it?'

'Love one, thank you.'

It was champagne, of course, and before they drank it he toasted their future together, then drew her down beside him on the sofa. The iron stove had been lit and the dim glow from the kitchen gave the only light as they drank their champagne and watched an enormous smoky moon rise out of the sea.

'Specially laid on,' Conal teased.

She laughed and said, 'Well, in that case, I'll have one every night I'm here. For ever.'

He grinned and told her she was greedy. It gave her a singing, fantastic delight to be here with him, to joke, to talk quietly and watch as he very efficiently cooked a delectable Chinese meal.

'No fortune cookies, I'm afraid,' he told her at the end. 'But I know what your fortune is going to be.'

'Tell me.'

His smile was lazily knowledgeable as he pulled her down to sit on the rug at his feet while he leaned back into the warm embrace of the sofa. 'Oh, happiness,' he said, the lightness of his tone failing to hide the intensity of emotion with which he spoke. 'And a very, very loving husband. Later some children if you want them.'

'I never thought I'd have children,' Catlin said dreamily, resting her cheek against his knees while her eyes watched the ever-changing patterns in the flames. Blue and green and purple from the salt in the driftwood, scarlet and rose and gold, they leapt and danced in the open maw of the heater.

'You may have as many as you like.'

She laughed at his grandiloquent tone. 'Well, as we've already got one to start with, we just might call a halt at a couple more. I'm glad Jenny likes me.'

'I'm glad you like her. She needs you.'

'Did you ever think that we'd get this far?' she asked suddenly.

His fingers had been playing with the thick amber tresses, moving through the clinging silk with loving gentleness. Now they stilled. After a long moment's silence he said quietly, 'I suppose I hoped all along, or why would I have insisted that you come back? I knew I had to see you, and it was more than just the desire to make sure that you were coping.'

Another long silence during which he wound a lock of hair around his forefinger. Almost absently he resumed, 'When you came into my room the night before you left me and began abusing me I was sickened and shamed by the fact that you'd seen us. I brought you here to kill those memories with other happier ones.'

It was easy enough to answer the unspoken question. 'Well, you've done that,' she said. 'Very much so.' Somewhat to her surprise she realised that it was the truth. Belinda Scargill no longer had the power to torment her; she could meet her tomorrow and feel only sympathy for her, and for Moya and for any other who had meant so little to Conal.

Wryly Conal said, 'I'm glad. Guilt and shame made me cruel. I lashed out and you got in the way. I wanted to show you I could be kind, too.'

He paused, but when she said nothing resumed, 'When I took you that first time I let you run back into your room because I thought any attempt on my part to comfort you would only have made things worse. Obviously that was a mistake.' That dry, self-mocking note hardened his voice. 'Call me conceited if you like, but I didn't believe that what had happened was so distasteful to you that it would force you to run away. I was sure you'd realise that the pain was only temporary.'

'I did,' she whispered. 'Oh, Conal, it wasn't that that made me run away! Deep down I've always known that what happened wasn't only your fault. I goaded you; looking back I can see that it was quite deliberate. What I couldn't forgive was your unfaithfulness. I wasn't going to be just one of your women, the legal one.' His fingers slid to her shoulders. As he hauled her up on to his knee she whispered, 'And I couldn't forgive myself for surrendering to you so *wantonly*! I thought I was abnormal.'

'So you ran away and deliberately turned yourself into a replica of Belinda just to show me.' His voice was heavy with self-disgust.

Biting her lip, Catlin looked up into the bleak planes and angles of his beloved face. With a delicate finger she traced the hard, exciting outline of his lips, the narrow springing arches of his brows, the strength of cheek and jawbone.

'Well, actually, no,' she confessed rather shame-facedly. 'Unless you could call a few kisses and some light petting gaining experience.'

The long lashes which had drooped in sensual appreciation of her caress lifted, revealing blue flames. '*What* did you say?'

She kissed him, mumbling against his mouth, 'I couldn't get over this thing about being married, you see. I lied to you.'

Beneath her hand his chest rose and fell as he drew a deep breath. '*No* lovers?'

'No lovers. Never. The chap on the phone is Deb's latest.'

'You terrify me,' he said with sombre intensity, 'by George, you do!'

'Why?'

'Because you know just where to aim your arrows! You'll never realise how much I've agonised over those non-existent affairs of yours.' A wry, self-deprecating smile touched his lips. 'If you wanted revenge for my women you've had it! The thought of you in another man's arms was bad enough, but I reasoned that you could only have done such violence to your principles because I'd crippled you emotionally. And that was worse!'

'But you loved me in spite of those non-existent lovers?'

The broad shoulders moved in a slight shrug.

'What does love have to do with common sense?' Conal asked a little bitterly. 'Of course I loved you regardless of how many men I thought you'd been to bed with. I love you because you're kind and generous and quick-tempered, intelligent and practical and stubborn, and because you laugh at the same things as I, and because whenever I set eyes on you, or think of you, or hear your voice, my whole being wants to be near you and within, joined so closely in every possible way that nothing can ever come between us again.'

As he spoke he moved, and Catlin found herself gently but inexorably borne down to the heavy woven fleece of the rug while he framed her face, holding it so that he could see the colour flood her skin. His smile was taunting yet tender and he bent his head to speak into her ear, his breath warmly erotic.

'Especially when I hear you moan your desire,' he said on a note of satisfaction. 'You have such a sweet, throaty warm voice for making love. Such a fiery, tempestuous——'

His mouth reached hers, seducing, lighting flames deep within her which set every nerve and vein throbbing. Catlin ran her hands down his body, wincing as the muscles hardened beneath her touch, her own body tense with excitement.

'Darling,' he whispered as she arched her throat, demanding the dangerous warmth of his touch there. 'Oh, dear Cat, I love you so!'

For once he was vulnerable, her need mirrored in the blue blaze of his gaze as he trembled in her arms.

'Yes, love me,' she moaned. Lost in the magic of his touch and the aching, burning response he aroused in her, she was at last free from the old memories. They no longer had the power to hurt.

Between the two of them they would make new memories with a sweetness and joy which would overlay the pain of those which had kept her company for so long, until the sting was gone from them entirely.

Outside the wind began to blow, but inside there were only soft murmurs and the lovely glow of firelight on two people whose long travels had at last led them to their journey's end.

Harlequin® Plus

A WORLD ABOUT THE AUTHOR

Robyn Donald cannot remember ever being unable to read. She learned the skill at a very early age; and today, she claims, reading remains one of her great pleasures, "if not a vice."

Robyn, her husband and their two children make their home in a small country village in the historic Bay of Islands in the far north of New Zealand. Both the climate and the people are friendly, and her family enjoys sailing in particular and the outdoor life in general.

Her other interests include cooking, music and astronomy. And she finds history and archaeology especially fascinating because "they are about the sum total of human experience."

When she writes, Robyn visualizes scenes that she knows and loves. The actual germ of a story arrives "ready-made from some recess of my brain, but," she adds, "it takes quite a while to work out the details!"

HARLEQUIN
PREMIERE AUTHOR EDITIONS

6 top Harlequin authors — 6 of their best books

1. JANET DAILEY Giant of Mesabi
2. CHARLOTTE LAMB Dark Master
3. ROBERTA LEIGH Heart of the Lion
4. ANNE MATHER Legacy of the Past
5. ANNE WEALE Stowaway
6. VIOLET WINSPEAR The Burning Sands

Harlequin is proud to offer these 6 exciting romance novels by 6 of our most popular authors. In brand-new beautifully designed covers, each Harlequin Premiere Author Edition is a bestselling love story—a contemporary, compelling and passionate read to remember!

Available wherever paperback books are sold, *or* through Harlequin Reader Service. Simply complete and mail the coupon below.

Harlequin Reader Service
In the U.S.
P.O. Box 52040
Phoenix, Ariz., 85072-9988

In Canada
649 Ontario Street
Stratford, Ontario N5A 6W2

Please send me the following editions of **Harlequin Premiere Author Editions**
I am enclosing my check or money order for $1.95 for each copy ordered, plus 75¢ to cover postage and handling.

☐ 1   ☐ 2   ☐ 3   ☐ 4   ☐ 5   ☐ 6

Number of books checked_____ @ $1.95 each = $_____
N.Y. state and Ariz. residents add appropriate sales tax $_____
Postage and handling $_____.7

TOTAL $_____

I enclose $_____
(Please send check or money order. We cannot be responsible for cash sent through the mail.) Price subject to change without notice.

NAME_____
(Please Print)
ADDRESS_____ APT. NO._____
CITY_____
STATE/PROV._____ ZIP/POSTAL CODE_____
Offer expires April 30, 1984

PA-W

3105600000

PASSIONATE!
CAPTIVATING!
SOPHISTICATED!

Harlequin Presents...

**The favorite fiction
of women the world over!**

Beautiful contemporary romances that
touch every emotion of a woman's heart—
passion and joy, jealousy and heartache...
but most of all...love.

Fascinating settings in the exotic
reaches of the world—
from the bustle of an international capital
to the paradise of a tropical island.

**All this and much, much more
in the pages of**

Harlequin Presents...

Wherever paperback books are sold, or through
Harlequin Reader Service

In the U.S.	In Canada
1440 South Priest Drive	649 Ontario Street
Tempe, AZ 85281	Stratford, Ontario N5A 6W2

**No one touches the heart of a woman
quite like Harlequin!**